# Eye of the Bird

## (A Quasi - Science Fiction)

**SIDDHANT GVALANI**

This book is dedicated to special persons in my life


*My family ….. My world*


*My Mom*

*Myomi, as I call her — the centre of my universe*


*My Dad*

*For whom I can do no wrong*


*Aanchal & Jay*

*I am the apple of their eye*


*Akash*

*Who is my greatest supporter — in a home away from home*

# CONTENTS

# ACKNOWLEDGEMENTS

*Writing this book was a rite of passage for me.*

*It was a combination of my interaction with so many people who*

*In some way or the other have touched the chords of inspiration.*

*Self-belief comes from the belief of people around us...*

*My parents: Mehak and Dr Anil Gvalani*

*My siblings: Akash, Aanchal & Jay*

*My extended family; the Mehta's; Gvalani's; and Hiduja's*

*My teachers at my Alma Mater: both Campion school and KC College*

*My Professors at Virginia Tech*

*My mentor: Babu*

*My Ex-principal, Dr Hemlata Bagla at KC College who always motivated me*

*My friends at Virginia Tech and in Mumbai*

*And above all my grandfather – who seeks the spark in me*

*I remain indebted to each one of you*

# PRELUDE: EYE OF THE BIRD

The grand Indian epic, the Mahabharata, unfolds a tale of intricate family rivalries and moral dilemmas set against the backdrop of a kingdom torn by ambition and power struggles. At its core are two branches of the royal lineage, the Pandavas and the Kauravas, vying for supremacy over the throne of Hastinapur.

The saga begins with the love story of Shantanu, the first king of Hastinapur, and Satyavati, a woman with a mysterious past. From her previous marriage to the sage Parashar, Satyavati bore a son named Vyasa, who would play a pivotal role in shaping the destiny of the Kuru dynasty. To secure her lineage's claim to the throne, Satyavati orchestrated the birth of heirs through Vyasa with the queens of Hastinapur, leading to the births of Dhritarashtra, Pandu, and Vidur. Pandu ascended the throne but was burdened by an ancient curse that rendered him unable to father children naturally. Through divine intervention, his queen conceived sons with various deities, resulting in the birth of the Pandavas: Yudhishthira, Bhima, Arjuna, Nakula, and Sahadeva.

Meanwhile, Dhritarashtra and his wife Gandhari had numerous children – (again through divine intervention), the infamous Kauravas led by Duryodhana. The princes were raised under the tutelage of teachers like Kripa and Dronacharya, where both camaraderie and enmity developed among them. As the princes came of age, tensions escalated, culminating in a public exhibition of their skills, where deep-seated animosities between the Pandavas and Kauravas were laid bare. Duryodhana, the eldest Kaurava, tried—and failed—to poison Bhima, the second Pandava.

Karna, the illegitimate son of Kunti, allied himself with Duryodhana due to his rivalry with Arjuna in archery. During the exhibition, Karna, though uninvited, challenged Arjuna but was insulted for his non-royal birth. In response, Duryodhana crowned Karna king of a vassal state on the spot.

The enmity between the Pandavas and Kauravas eventually escalated into the epic battle of the Mahabharata, with the Kauravas fighting for power and the Pandavas for justice.

Initially, Arjuna was reluctant to fight, knowing the slaughter that would occur among his own relatives on the enemy side. However, his charioteer and close friend, Lord Krishna, persuaded him otherwise. Their dialogue on the issues of war—courage, duty, the nature of life and the soul, and the role of the Gods—forms the Bhagavad Gita, one of the key episodes in the Mahabharata.

Arjuna, known for his deep sense of duty, was also sensitive and thoughtful, as demonstrated by his misgivings about the Kurukshetra war. His lifelong rapport with

Krishna guided him through these dilemmas. His dedication to his duty was so profound that he once chose exile rather than refusing to help a Brahmin in need.

Dronacharya, revered as both a great teacher and warrior, strongly influenced Indian social traditions and inspired debates about morality and dharma in the Mahabharata. Among all the Kaurava and Pandava brothers, Arjuna emerged as the most dedicated and naturally talented under Drona's tutelage, even surpassing Drona's own son Ashwatthama. Arjuna's devotion to his teacher impressed Drona, who recognized his pupil's potential.

Arjuna's prowess as a warrior was established early in his life. He diligently learned everything Dronacharya could teach, earning the status of "Maharathi" or outstanding warrior.

A famous anecdote from their training illustrates Arjuna's focus and skill. Drona once tested his students by hanging a wooden bird from a tree branch and asked each to aim for the bird's eye. When asked what they saw, most students described the surroundings, the tree, and the bird itself. However, when Drona asked Arjuna what he saw, Arjuna replied, "I see the eye of the bird."

This anecdote, often recounted, symbolized Arjuna's unwavering focus and determination—qualities that would define his journey through the epic battle that lay ahead.

# Chapter 1

# GUNS OF NAVARONE: MY STINT AT RIFLE SHOOTING…

Rifle shooting as a sport seemed to stimulate me.

Just as Arjuna saw the eye of the bird, I could only see the perfect ten mark on the target. Pressing the butt onto my shoulder, resting the grip onto my left palm, and gazing into the scope. The feeling was simply ecstatic.

However, the human body is built to move.

The feeling of restlessness sets in - every fifteen seconds. An itchy calf, hatefully hearing the fan's whirring noise…, seeing the mobile constantly to know if she texted you back, watching the second-hand move-tik-tok….

We humans are bound to be taken away from the zen-like state we seek to maintain. The world is wired to take your eye away from the eye of the bird. The focus. The "Lakshya".

My attention span generally lasted about three minutes.

I remember last summer; I visited the Met Museum and I stared into a painting of the Mona Lisa.

First minute: "Oh how detailed her eyes are. Why are they following me?"

I am near the big Chinese Ling vase but…., they're still on me. I'm talking to a friend on call. They're still on me! I've digressed from Da Vinci to Picasso. Mona Lisa's eyes are still on me...

Second minute: "Oh how frizzy her hair is. Surely Da Vinci wanted to bring out her average appearance and make her seem like one of us. To probably indicate that there can be something extraordinary in the ordinary? Her smile was simply so mysterious…

"It is almost as if motion and emotion are intertwining." I thought and looked away, and her smile changed... or so I felt.

Third minute I wondered to myself: "How was her attention span so long. I've been all over the Met, but her eyes were glued to me. If only I could be her and watch one thing for so long." Fourth minute: "Met.. I am out of here. Mona Lisa has given me a severe complex."

Today, I learned that Mona Lisa was who I strived to be. The single-minded focus. I found that her eyes were so hell bent on making you think what she's thinking. I had a dream of her one night, where she was looking at me for a while and suddenly, she looked away. I woke up. That was the sort of convergence that made one go crazy. I imagined having a mind like hers.

If I did, I would be hitting the ten mark every single attempt.

At the museum I had read that Leonardo's mastery allowed him to craft a smile on the Mona Lisa that eluded direct capture, appearing only when we aren't too fixated on finding it. In simple words – the less the focus, the greater the famous enigmatic smile would charm and reach out to you……

By meticulously detailing the subtle lines at the corners of her mouth, he created a slight downturn, mirroring the anatomical precision found in his sketches. When one stared directly at her mouth, the retina picked up these minute intricacies, seemingly negating any smile.

However, when the gaze shifted slightly away from the mouth to other features like her eyes or cheeks, then the mouth was only seen peripherally. In this peripheral view, the shadows gave the impression of her lips turning upwards into a gentle smile. AH! What showcasing of Leonardo's skilful manipulation of perception and detail. Lose focus to see it. But I knew I could not be Leonardo. I had to be like Mona Lisa whose focus was so sharp that it seemed to bore into your very being.

So, is that what made the Mona Lisa so special? The mysterious smile, the rosy cheeks, and the frizzy hair? Beauty lies in the eyes of the beholder. I saw beauty in her eyes. Mona Lisa did not have an attention span as short as mine. She was so calm and composed. I never saw her restless. I never saw her itchy or checking herself out in her camera. I only ever saw oil dripping down the canvas of her face.

Perhaps, an underlying message Da Vinci was trying to convey to us painting enthusiasts was to neglect everything unimportant. Blur the unnecessary in life.

Maybe he was trying to provoke us to look at what is important: yourself.

I realize Mona Lisa would probably be the best rifle shooter in the world. The gaze, the focus, the confidence. Her vibe screamed a perfect ten. Although, I don't think she would look as pretty in the painting with a gun in her hand.

I remember gazing into the scope of my rifle and thinking of hitting the perfect 10.

And I did succeed!

However, my instructor wasn't as impressed as I was.

"Siddhant, do not hunch your back. Legs should be shoulder-width apart.

Additionally, I hear you breathing too fast. Calm your nerves."

"But Prof., I hit the ten."

"If you're form isn't correct, you will hit the perfect ten just once out of ten times."

I proceeded to take nine more shots. My instructor was wrong: I hit the perfect ten once more in those nine attempts. In hindsight, I should have controlled my breathing. Why exactly is breathing so important in rifle shooting? With the gun in your hand, one eye squint and the other closed, one would think it is just a matter of pulling the trigger. However, breathing while firing the shot hurts accuracy because it increases the movement of the aligned sights on the target (wobble area).

So, your respiration can affect your eyesight. Now, I wanted to be the best shooter in the world.

How does the best shooter in the world control his/ her respiration?

I sought to try yoga. I remember visiting my high school yoga instructor and asking her, "ma'am how do I breathe better than the rest?"

She was startled. "How do you breathe better than the rest? I do not quite understand your dilemma, Sid."

I told her how I wanted to be the best shooter in the world and, my breathing affected my abilities to shoot. She told me to practice 'Pranayama': an exercise in which controlling your breath could control the power of your mind.

She said that yogic breathing exercises can help you control your life force, also known as the prana. My yoga teacher then went on to saying that Prā is more than just breath. She stressed specifically on "Samān", or balancing the digestive system. Fasting I guessed - as it was responsible for digestion. A form of self-discipline.

Well, in India, fasting has long been practiced as a spiritual technique, rooted in the understanding that diet influences one's character and behaviour. By restricting food intake, the senses are weakened, and "Samān", which governs digestion, is forced to balance itself.

I thought to myself: fasting cannot be too hard. Compensating on food sounds fair – considering that I wanted to be the best shooter in the world. I fasted from 6 am – 6pm. Basically when the sun was out. My friends are all Muslim and during Ramadan, they do the same. I wondered what it would be like being in their shoes.

I remembered my friend Awais fasted for thirty days straight and fell so ill that he landed up in a hospital. But then he is not the devout religious fellow like the others were. He was a real adventurer. I couldn't help but imagine how hungry he must have been by the end!

I know I got irritable enough if I missed a single meal, so going thirty days with limited food sounded like a real-life waking nightmare. I could picture poor Awais by day ten, already looking like a hungry extra from a zombie apocalypse movie. His stomach probably sounded like an angry velociraptor every time he walked by a McDonalds. Then after the two-week mark, when his body started burning through muscle instead of fat, Awais was probably wobbling around, weak as a kitten. I remembered him zoning out during conversations, drooling slightly while fantasizing about bathing in an infinite vat of mac and cheese. By the final week, he was surely delirious - desperately hallucinating - entire thanksgiving feasts appearing out of thin air in front of him. He probably tried to take a bite out of a throw pillow or two before finally admitting defeat against the extreme munchies. When Awais ended up in the hospital on an IV drip, I could imagine how heavenly that first sip of sugary rehydration fluid tasted to his starving body. He'd been thirty days without a single snack to satisfy his insatiable cravings - the guy deserved some kind of medal for that level of food deprivation!

I tried surviving a week with Awais' willpower. I remember I was so weak that I couldn't pick up my rifle! The second my instructor busted out a leftover pizza, I was a drooling, blubbering mess begging for the smallest morsel. "Pran" and Samān did me no good for, in as little as a week, I was starving.

Additionally, my breathing was the same. Maybe it worsened because every time I took a breath, I could smell that barbecue pizza that my instructor loved. How I wished....

I attempted to hit the perfect ten. I thought to myself, all that yajna had to account for a few perfect tens. I pressed the butt of the rifle against my shoulder, rested the grip upon my left palm and gazed into the scope. I pulled the trigger.

The pellet flew through thin air and.... missed the target.

Something had to change. I went home and ordered a barbecue pizza, from my favourite place to eat: Tony Baloney's Pizza. As I was eating the pizza, I thought to myself: the Bhagavad Gita cannot always be correct. I must contain my superstitions for, if they took over me, I would have no opinions of my own. Thereon, I resorted to forming my own ideas to be the best rifle shooter in the world.

*Firstly, take eight breaths before pulling the trigger.*

Why eight? Because it was my jersey number in high school soccer. And trust me I was poetry in motion on the field. Oh, how I loved playing wingback. I remember gliding through defences with the "Ronaldo cutback" and "Messi body faint." I could still hear the roar of the crowd as I received the ball wide on the flank, that crisp new adidas on my feet. With a couple of deft Ronaldo cutback moves,

I'd easily sashay past the first few defenders, their teenage legs never stood a chance against my magic footwork. Then as the burly centre-backs rushed out to close me down, it was time to deploy the Messi body faint - stopping on a dime before dipping that shoulder to send them haplessly sprawling past. The sweet smell of freshly cut grass lingered as the goal loomed ahead, an unblemished net beckoning.

With the keeper rooted, I'd pick that pinpoint top corner and unleashed a few dizzying steps before crackling the bending shot just inside the post.

Shambolic defensive line well and truly torn asunder by my individual brilliance!

The ref's whistle was drowned out by thunderous cheers as I sprinted away in celebration.

Those were the days my friends - a carefree existence of weaving magic on the pitch, idealized soccer highlights playing on an endless loop.

We were young kings ruling our favourite parks and concrete playing grounds with flair. Before life's stresses and responsibilities took hold, the beautiful game was the only thing that mattered. It also made me think that eight is my lucky number. Hence eight breaths before pulling the trigger.

*Secondly, to hold the trigger for a longer time, even after firing.*

This helped me reduce recoil. I remember once letting the trigger go and suffering a huge upward recoil. The pellet went and hit the roof of the shooting range. My instructor made me pay a fine of five hundred rupees for damaging his roof. My cheek was red as the butt of the gun nearly broke my cheekbone. I was bandaged for a week. The fine itself wasn't as hurtful as my friends' laughter.

They had always been better than me. I told them of my dream of being the best shooter in the world and how I fasted for a week to achieve it. My friend Ronald replied, "My brother, if you don't eat those greens, you're not going to be able to lift the rifle." He was right. Ronald was the "Abhinav Bindra" of my shooting range. He just could not stop hitting the ten. My instructor once gave him his "India coat" – the one that he wore to the commonwealth games in Delhi in 2012. Seeing Ronald in the orange, white, and green hit a nerve in my body that I have never felt before. I could not explain the feeling. It was a realization that I wanted to wear the coat but could not because I wasn't skilful enough as Ronald.

Jealousy too. One day, I sneaked into his locker by stealing his keys. I put on the coat, looked in the mirror and realized how ridiculous I looked.

"Me? representing India? Haha Imagine instructor Savarkar seeing this." The worst part was that Ronald caught me wearing his coat. I thought he would get me out of the academy by telling instructor Savarkar. But no, instead, he gave me a message for life: "Sid, the fruit of your labour will taste sweeter when the labour is yours. Not anyone else's. I have worked my backside off for the coat. Hard work isn't easy. Gazing into the scope at three in the morning isn't easy. But the thought of wearing that coat makes me think everything is worth it."

My jealousy turned into genuine appraisal for Ronald at that instant. A boy who was so successful and humble deserved nothing but applause. I yearned to be a Ronald.

Maybe by following instructor Savarkar's ways, and not sniffing for pizzas, I could be a Ronald.

*Thirdly, take at least thirty seconds to pull the trigger from the time I lay my cheek on the butt of the gun. In other words, slow down.*

Several years ago, at an instructional event hosted by Springfield Armory on a rainy San Diego Day, I had the privilege of receiving guidance from one of the sports' living legends – Rob Leatham. Among the many valuable pointers he imparted - one drill for honing accuracy had become a regular part of my practice regimen. The concept was deceptively simple: set up a blank target without any bullseye or aiming point at a close distance (5 yards for handguns, 25 for rifles). Take my stance, find my sight picture on the centre of mass and squeeze off one controlled shot. Then, the real challenge began. Taking as much time as needed between each subsequent shot, fire the remainder of your magazine with the sole objective of shooting through that original bullet hole without allowing the group to expand outwards.

On its surface, this seemed like a straightforward exercise. However, those who have attempted it could attest to just how difficult and humbling an endeavour it was. There was simply no room for even a miniscule error in sight alignment, breath control, or trigger press. The slightest flinch or lapse in fundamentals would pull your rounds outside of that solitary hole, making this a "slow fire."

Drill forces you to bring your complete and unwavering focus to each shot. So, what was the purpose behind such an exacting practice method? As Leatham explained, it reinforced and ingrained the proper muscle memory and mechanics for accurate marksmanship at its most basic level. When you can consistently achieve one tight unbroken hole at close range, your fundamentals are truly locked in. From that solid foundation, you can proceed to incrementally greater distances (moving to 10 yards for handguns, 50 for rifles) and apply that same discipline. Mastering a flinchless trigger press is perhaps the biggest obstacle faced by shooters of all levels.

In essence, Rob Leatham had conceived an elegant exercise that returned me to the pure fundamentals to identify my weaknesses and solidify my strengths. By removing the crutches of marked targets and dialling in on that solitary aiming point, the emphasis was squarely on perfecting sight picture, breath control, trigger control, and developing a steady, unperturbed shooting foundation. It was a practice method that required discipline, patience, focus - the same qualities that epitomize true marksmanship. For those seeking to take their accuracy to the highest level, this "one hole" drill was certainly worth the effort. Rob 'Arjuna' Leatham to the rescue.

What is it about rifle shooting that excited me? The smell of the lead covered barrel? The sweet sound the chamber made when I locked it in? Or loading a pallet into the breech? None of these. To me, rifle shooting was seen as more than just hitting a spot on a target. It was an escape from the mundane world. Up at 7AM, catching the bus to school, sitting through physics class- "RIGHT children, gravitational potential energy equals mass times acceleration due to gravity times….." could all get monotonous after the 10-year grind.

But then I'd think of the smell of the gunpowder and the ritual of carefully unloading my weapon to study the intricate inner workings of the rifle. That brought me solace.

After the final bell, instead of heading straight home to eat lunch with my sister, I'd take the bus from the end of our street - a 15-minute walk - to the stop opposite a place called Shivaji Park. This name resonated with me so deeply because it was named after the legendary Shivaji Maharaj, ruler of the Maratha dynasty, who embodied warrior devotion and principles like the epic hero Arjuna. In fact, Shivaji himself was inspired by the stories from the Mahabharata that his mother would read to him as a child, not unlike how my own mother would recite scripture passages like the divine Gayatri Mantra to me.

Those sacred verses brought out the very essence of a mother's unconditional love for her child. And yet, as poetic as those bonding moments were, I couldn't escape my mom's constant refrains of "Stop sitting on your phone, you nalayak!" Nalayak meaning essentially "good for nothing" in her scolding hierarchy of terms.

But when I arrived at Shivaji Park, grabbed my rifle, and took my position at the firing range, everything else simply melted away. The aromas of the smokeless powder, the methodical cadence of loading and unloading, finding my rhythm between breaths - it all became a transporting meditation. In those moments, I wasn't a distracted student weighed down by exam stress or filial guilt. I was a successor to the determined warriors of lore, focused solely on mastering an ancient skill that demanded presence of mind, spiritual fortitude, and a unity of breath and bullet.

My own private escape from the mundane into a realm of heritage and higher callings.

So, while the smells, sounds and actions of rifle shooting held pleasures of their own, they were largely symbolic gateways to a deeper state of contemplation and connection to ethnic identity. A much-needed refuge from the relentless pull of adolescent restlessness and societal pressures.

One day, I was watching the Olympics with my mother. We witnessed India's pistol shooters losing to the American competitors round after round. As she lamented "Where have the Abhinav Bindras of this sport disappeared?", a fire burned within me. For some reason, I felt an overwhelming urge to prove to her that I was not just some slacker sitting around the house doing nothing. That's when I joined the Savarkar Academy Air Rifle Training Program. I could feel the weight and expectations on my shoulders as all eyes poured into me during those first sessions. But as soon as I let that first pellet fly and watched it strike the 10 ring, something awakened.

On September 2nd, 2022, exactly one year after confiding in my mother about my aspirations, I managed to hit the 10 ring an incredible 20 times consecutively with her watching proudly from the stands.

Surely one would think my instructor, the venerable Sarkar Prof., would be suitably impressed by such a feat from his student. But no - the very next day on September 3rd, his only critique was that my feet weren't set wide enough in my stance. I'll admit, in that youthful moment of arrogance, I hated him for not simply rating me as the best shooter in the academy right then and there. It took some time, but I eventually realized Savarkar Prof. was right, and I was wrong.

In life, there was always room for improvement, be it baking a chocolate cake or vying to win the Olympic gold for your country. For me and my enduring love of rifle shooting, it wasn't just my leg stance that needed refinement, but also my ability to accept being second best.

We Sagittarians can indeed be quite egoistic by nature. It's true - I am quite blunt - to a fault at times. I even once candidly told a friend that her looks were not the kind to launch a thousand ships. She didn't take it well, but I've never shied away from harsh truths. I often cross the line between radical honesty and unintentionally hurting people's feelings. In retrospect with my friend, I could have been just as honest by saying she simply wasn't my preferred type, rather than uttering an insensitive remark.

I used this same blunt attitude to finally muster the courage to tell Savarkar Prof. that I deserved to be awarded the prestigious India colour's blazer. To my surprise, he agreed with my self-appraisal, but applied a condition - I would need to defeat his protege Ronald Scott in a 20-shot match before being awarded the blazer. At first, I scoffed at the proposed challenge.

Surely, I was not that far below Ronald's level. Probably my instructor potentially saw in me a capability that would place myself in the same league as Ronald? However, I knew there had to be some deeper strategic reason for Savarkar Prof. issuing such a trial.

After all, this was the same sagely man who, despite winning a silver medal at the 2012 Commonwealth Games, held an admirably Zen-like acceptance of not capturing gold. To me, that sense of satisfaction regardless of the ultimate outcome revealed a profound wisdom and sagaciousness. It made me question why Savarkar Prof. himself had never pushed to compete at the Olympics and represent India on the highest stage.

When I asked him about this, he revealed that around 2015, he had tragically lost his wife in a devastating car accident. The emotional trauma and toll on his mental health caused him to miss out on qualifying for the 2016 Rio Olympics despite being in prime form. The Indian rifle association ultimately dropped him from the national team in 2017 after he failed to finish in the top 15 at the selection events.

His dream of representing the country on sport's biggest stage died there.

I empathized with Savarkar Prof.'s heartbreaking story, but nonetheless urged him that it's never too late to rekindle that Olympic-level passion and hunger if it still burned within him. He admired my undying optimism but accepted that that particular flame had long been extinguished. The only path forward was to impart his knowledge on the next generation of shooters like Ronald and myself.

As Savarkar Prof. gazed jointly at Ronald and me, I knew we were all on the same page - this mentor-student showdown would be the catalysing crucible to elevate one of us while providing closure on his own unfulfilled dreams. Finally, my "Rocky" moment was about to begin.

The event would take place with the standard 10m air rifle discipline used in most major competitions since the 1984 Los Angeles Olympics. The 4.5mm calibre air rifles weigh around 5kg, with the bulk of the weight distributed towards the rear to help balance the weapon and mitigate recoil.

Heading into the match, I made some key adjustments to my technique and equipment based on Savarkar Prof.'s insights. I gripped the rifle slightly farther forward than usual to better balance the weight over the centre of mass, allowing a more upright and stable shooting posture. I widened my stance as instructed, absorbing the downward force through my legs and hips. And critically, I invested in one of the modern pre-charged pneumatic air rifle designs that minimized shot-to-shot variation with their recoilless, vibration-free performance.

Thanks to the refinements, I no longer needed to labour through an elongated trigger pull to avoid destabilizing the weapon. My groupings were tighter and more consistent than ever before without fliers or stray rounds being inevitably sprayed.

The balance and ergo dynamics helped maintain that crucial straight line between my body, the sights, and the target. Savarkar Prof.'s adjustments had elevated me into a more complete, technically proficient shooter - one finally capable of challenging his former protege. He knew it, but now it was simply up to me to validate his teachings and claim what was rightfully mine.

The stage was set for an epic showdown.

On the morning of the match, my mother prepared me a simple but symbolic breakfast - badaam, or almonds and yoghurt. In Hindu traditions, almonds play an integral role in prayer offerings and are commonly gifted during festivals like Diwali and Holi to confer blessings and good fortune. I'm not normally a superstitious person, but I decided that day to embrace the spiritual significance. If consuming those sacred nuts could imbue me with whatever mental or cosmic edge was needed to overcome Ronald, I would indulge those beliefs wholeheartedly.

You can call it irrational, but I've always been of the mindset that believing you can accomplish something is already half the battle. I took the bus to our usual haunt of Shivaji Park. As I entered the range, I locked eyes with Ronald, who sardonically sported the prestigious India team blazer I coveted - no doubt trying to throw me off my game and reassert his dominance. But my mind was utterly locked in on one thing and one thing only out-duelling him to finally claim the symbolic colours that I felt were rightfully mine.

As the familiar scent of smokeless powder wafted through the still morning air, I stood united with my breath and began my relentless pursuit of the perfect 10. We each grasped our rifles firmly, taking our positions on the firing line as Sarkar Prof. barked out the final instructions. "You'll have one minute to fire a single shot at the target. Get set... Fire!"

The opening rounds were remarkably even, with Ronald and I trading perfect 10s back and forth like gunslingers locked in a tense stare down. Around the 10th shot we were still deadlocked, but I could feel the pressure mounting with each exhaled breath hanging heavier in the range air.

By the 14th shot my mind momentarily wavered, and I missed the 10 ring for the first time. "It's over," I thought dejectedly, "Ronald doesn't miss in his sleep."

But to my surprise, the smug favourite flinched on the very next shot, spraying a stray 9 to surrender his narrow lead as we reached the final sprint. Approaching the climactic 20th round, I held a one ring advantage over my adversary. Savarkar Prof. leaned in and urged firmly, "Just one more, fire when ready..." Those 50 eternal seconds stretched into a lifetime as I settled into my stance. Legs precisely shouldered, rifle level and pressing into my raised shooting arm, left elbow braced onto the fat of my hip, I was a breath away from actuating the perfect trigger squeeze to potentially claim my destiny. But then it struck me - I had failed to observe my own sacred pre-shot routine of eight stabilizing inhalations!

In a panic, I gulped one frantic breath and desperately snapped the trigger in a flurry of motion. The recoil barely registered as the errant pellet sailed hopelessly wide. My anguished eyes instantly snapped to Ronald, whose steely calm had not abandoned him in the clutch. The vindicated victor steadied, exhaled, and squeezed off the decisive 10.3 ring to snatch the victory from my flailing grasp.

As tears of frustration and failure welled in my eyes, my life's ambition disappeared from my trembling grasp in a shattering instant - all because of a single missed breath cycle. That autonomic, natural process I had taken for granted proved to be my undoing when it mattered most.

In that gut-wrenching moment, the cold truth washed over me like a harsh monsoon downpour. Deep down, I knew I had crumbled under the intense pressure of the situation. It was nobody's shortcoming but my own lack of composure that robbed me of glory. The feelings of regret and self-loathing led me to hastily discard my expensive competition rifle as if ridding myself of the very instrument that had betrayed my dreams.

As the despair consumed me, the last person I expected consolation from was Savarkar Prof. himself. He approached with an expression more of restrained pride than pity. "Shabash," he said matter-of-factly, invoking the deeply resonant Hindi word of praise and encouragement. Every Indian child is intimately familiar with that simple utterance and the profound sense of validation it conveys from a revered elder, mentor or parent. The first time I felt that swell of accomplishment was over a decade ago as a gangly 12-year-old.

On one particularly dreary Friday evening when venturing out was prohibited by the heavy rains, I had gotten it into my head to surprise my father by baking him a cheesecake from scratch. Despite my predictably disastrous first attempt resulting in a mangled, flavourless mess, he didn't scold or rebuke. Instead, he simply patted his belly with a contented smile and warmly declared "Shabash" - his understated way of saying "I'm proud of you for trying."

With those two weighty syllables, I realized Savarkar Prof. was genuinely appreciative that I hadn't shied away from the crucible. While I may have faltered and fallen short of the goal, he seemed to view the very act of chasing that dream as a powerful first step in forging the temper of my character and commitment. He then offered the seasoned perspective that "failure is only a steppingstone to success." My mother too was ecstatic with my performance. The last miss made not an iota of difference to her. I was the genuine star of the moment for her. And she was not being subjective because I was her son. She saw my perseverance. It was through her and Prof. Savarkar that I suddenly felt enlightened - enabled to recognize that although I had not cleared the final bar, I had demonstrated an ability to at least occupy the same rarified air as someone of Ronald's prowess.

The sport of rifle shooting had indelibly taught me the vital lesson of being appreciative of the skills and presence of mind required to be second best. Bruce Lee once said "I have absolute confidence not in being number two, but in being number one." At first that may sound like an arrogant statement from the legendary martial artist. Like he's proclaiming he'll accept nothing less than being the very best. But then he followed it up with "But then I have enough sense to realize there can be no number one." This second part provides more context to his mindset. Bruce wasn't being boastful - he was acknowledging the inherent futility in obsessing over being declared the singular best at anything. No matter how skilled, dedicated or talented you may be, there will always be someone else out there working just as hard, if not harder than you. Someone pushing the boundaries of what's possible in that activity or discipline. As soon as you reach one peak of achievement, there will be a new mountain to climb, a new bar to raise.

Bruce Lee realized that fixating on being the undisputed, eternal "number one" was an exercise in vanity.

That no matter how masterful you become, that status will inevitably be questioned and challenged by others' abilities over time. There's always another young upstart looking to usurp the throne. So instead of wasting energy on claiming physical or ideological superiority over everyone else, Bruce Lee's philosophy focused on constantly evolving, transcending your previous limitations, and treating each endeavour as an ongoing self-mastery. Don't strive for the false idolatry of being number one. Have the confidence and self-assuredness to outwork and outperform yourself ad infinitum. There would always be another hungry young Turk out there, in another part of the world, at that very moment methodically applying their craft - savouring the smoky scent of each new pellet, tenderly loading the breech, centering the scope...and repeatedly scorching not 20, but an incomprehensible 50 consecutive bullseyes.

My own personal measuring stick of what constituted world-class greatness had been irreversibly expanded well beyond the confines of our humble Savarkar Academy halls. What I once considered the pinnacle of achievement was now clearly just a modest plateau on the infinite ascent towards true mastery.

While this may have been the terminus of my own fledgling journey, it was overwhelmingly apparent that rifle shooting occupied a much vaster stratosphere for professionals like Ronald. This was not merely a hobby or pastime to be equally prioritized amidst life's other demands and diversions. Rifle shooting was Ronald's singular obsession - his reason for rising at 3am to commence training while the world remained asleep and unburdened by such dedication to craft.

As for me, I had always harboured other indulged passions and pursuits beyond this discipline.

As I slowly made my way out of Shivaji Park clutching the spent rifle case under my trembling arm, I realized my dogged journey from that first spark of adolescent daydreaming to this crushing denial had reframed my entire perception of paths, destinations and the omnipresent space betwixt. Those dusty almanacs of wisdom and maxim no longer rang hollow - failure was merely a humbling correction, resetting one's spiritual odometer with a refilled perspective on just how far the road yet ahead still winds.

Rifle shooting was never meant to be my sole defining passion. Even from a young age, I had a wide array of hobbies and interests competing for my attention.

Whenever my parents asked if I preferred being outdoors or burying my head in textbooks, my answer constantly wavered. I vividly remember those carefree evenings where the pure joy of dribbling a soccer ball between the neighbourhood boys made the world feel perfect and timeless. Running barefoot on the rough ground, our shouts and laughter echoing through the streets until that fateful call would beckon me home as the sky purpled.

Then it was a dead sprint back to my second realm - the cozy embrace of indoor escapism. Breathlessly bounding through the doorway, abandoning my sweat-soaked shoes and quickly firing up the latest game console. I'd eagerly nest myself in my personal blanket fortress, the dull hum of the AC heavy in the air as I hugged my pillow tight and allowed my mind to be transported to warzones of the game 'Fortnite'. These simple pleasures - the physical thrill of athletics giving way to sedentary but imaginative coziness - brought me the deepest satisfaction. Despite my mother's entrepreneurial energy and zest, I've always naturally leaned towards the lethargic side of the pendulum. She seemingly wished I embodied more of her proactive zeal, but my curiosities gravitated towards the theoretical realms of reading, writing, and science.

I still fondly recall the lessons of our moustachioed physics teacher, Prof. Joaquin. With his bushy eyebrows and deep baritone voice, he effortlessly covered not just physics, but biology, computer science, math - he was a true renaissance educator. Sadly, even as a supposed "jack of all trades", this man faltered when it came to properly articulating the nuances of classical Newtonian physics. While the rest of us nibbled on our jammed bread-butters during snack break, Prof. Joaquin was always left scratching his head over the "P" in physics, and why exactly did that apple seem so determined to disobey the heavenly laws.

Those nostalgic images of blessed simplicity and childhood contradictions have remained emblazoned - tiny retorts to the notion that one's purpose must be quickly heeded and set in stone. For all my shooting exploits and tussles with gravitas, a part of me still longed for the simpler gratifications. Yet, out of all my varied hobbies and interests over the years, it was the quirky world of physics that ultimately unlocked and brought forth the very best in me as a curious, determined student of the universe's mysteries.

# Chapter 2

# ERNO'S CHALLENGE

Rifle shooting taught me two things: Whatever I decide to do in life must have the same precision as required in this sport. Ah! The single-minded attention, the discipline, and finally, the thrill of achieving the aim - all resonated deeply within me. But without precision, the goal would always be a "blur," never the focus.

I began looking for this quality in the simplest things—the design of a spider web and the orbital movement of a planet. One day, I stumbled upon a coloured cube. It amazed me how symmetrical it was. I began counting the colours on it: blue, red, yellow, green, white, orange. It was almost as if a rainbow afar was squeezed into being a 3-dimensional toy.

I grasped this cube and went to my father and asked him what was the real purpose of it. "Ah son! You have found the humble but challenging Rubik's Cube.

My first attempt at solving Erno Rubik's combination puzzle took me 17 hours of mind-numbing pain; eventually I gave up. Those clicks into place felt like a checkmate to mediocrity—a bullseye."

And I know how painful it can be to not achieve a bullseye. Not to mention the pain coming second to Ronald. But this "Rubik's Cube" bullseye explored a different part of my brain. I was amazed at how determined I was to perfect this cube.

My father is a man of science, a doctor of great renown. Whenever I visited DYP Hospital, nurses would greet him with reverence, "Namaste Saab," acknowledging his achievements – 143 successful surgeries, 70 lives brought back from the jaws of death, and tens of thousands of students taught over the years. He was not just a skilled surgeon but also a respected professor.

As I sat outside his classroom at DYP, I could hear his authoritative voice resonating through the halls, "Good morning, students. Today, we will be learning about tracheostomy. Air trapped under the emphysema can damage the oesophagus building up of air between the pneumothorax and chest wall can cause complications like hematoma and damage the tracheo-oesophageal fistula or tracheo-innominate fistula." He would rattle off complex terms with such ease that they sounded like intricate tongue twisters to my untrained ears. How did he memorize and understand such complex medical jargon? Apparently, medically inclined people love sophisticating things. Not my sister though.

She, also a brilliant doctor in the making, was among the students attending his lectures. One day, with a mischievous glint in her eye, she challenged him, "Could you elucidate the procedural protocol for performing a percutaneous tracheostomy intervention, elucidating the intricate intricacies of the incisional induction and the subsequent substructural subcutaneous subtleties that necessitate meticulous manipulation to mitigate potential postoperative pulmonary perturbations?" The class turned towards her, stunned by the complexity of her query, as if she were a reincarnation of Hippocrates himself. Yet, my father beamed with pride, yearning to exclaim, "That's my daughter!" Instead, he calmly answered her question, breaking down the intricate procedure step by step... "For performing a percutaneous tracheostomy, the initial step involves proper patient positioning and preoperative preparation of the intended puncture site. The clinician must palpate the anatomical landmarks to identify the optimal location for percutaneous access.

Next, a small incision is made through the skin and subcutaneous tissue layers to establish an entry point. Careful dissection and retraction of the underlying musculature and fascial planes is required to create a pathway to the trachea. Haemostasis must be achieved throughout the procedure to maintain a clear operative field. Once the tracheal rings are visualized, a needle is introduced into the tracheal lumen, followed by serial dilators to gradually enlarge the tract. The tracheostomy tube is then inserted into the established stoma, and the adjustable flanges are secured to stabilize the tube's positioning........"

As my father and sister engaged in this intellectual sparring, exchanging medical jargon with the fluency of a shared language, I felt like an outsider in my own family. While they competed in this battle of wits, challenging each other's grasp of complex terminology like "subcutaneous emphysema," "pneumothorax," and "tracheo-innominate fistula", my confused face and slightly agape mouth drew bewildered looks from passersby who must have wondered if I was amid an existential crisis.

"You'll catch a fly or two like that my friend."

My family seemed gifted with an abundance of intellectual prowess, as if destined for their own reality show, "Keeping Up with the Gvalanis." But I was the unique child, possessing a different kind of intelligence – resilience and determination. As I sat cross-legged on the floor, staring intently at the Rubik's Cube, I saw it not as a toy but as a portal to unlocking the secrets of the universe. With a deep breath, I began twisting and turning the cube, the colours blurring in a kaleidoscopic frenzy – blue, red, green, white, blue, white, red, yellow, green, blue, white, orange, green, orange, red, white, orange, blue, red, yellow, white.

Sweat beaded on my furrowed brow as I worked through the algorithms and formulae, scribbling furiously on a whiteboard with notations like "Face 3, Column 3, turn up, face 2 row 1 turn left, face 1 row 1 turn left, face 6 column 3 turn down"

My determination was unwavering, fuelled by the desire to conquer this challenge, to prove my intellect transcended mere medical jargon. My room resembled an MIT student's laboratory, equations and diagrams covering every inch of the walls. In the centre sat the maddening Rubik's cube, taunting me with its chaotic mosaic of colours. I had been working on it for hours, obsessively twisting and turning the rows in search of patterns. The first glimmer of progress emerged as a cross of white squares formed on the bottom face. A small victory, but one that ignited my determination.

I envisioned building similar crosses on each face, unifying the colours into harmonious patterns. However, the cube proved far more complex than I anticipated, its combinations seemingly infinite.

Frustration mounted, so I implemented a strategy of 25-minute work periods followed by five minute breaks. During those precious respites, I indulged in YouTube videos about the Hungarian. I pored over every biographical detail, desperate to unlock the secrets lurking within his brilliant mind. The statistics were staggering - this unassuming plastic toy contained a staggering 43,252,003,274,489,856,000 potential arrangements!

Only one configuration was the elusive "solved" state I so feverishly sought. I couldn't help but wonder if Rubik's own children, now likely middle-aged themselves, possessed some profound insight into their father's creation.

In the Mahabharata, Arjuna would close his eyes, visualizing his targets with laser- like clarity before releasing his arrows. I decided to emulate this practice, squeezing my eyes shut and allowing the cube's geometry to imprint itself onto my mind's eye. At first, all I perceived was chaos. But slowly, subtly, the individual planes began aligning into larger symmetrical patterns. The vision solidified – to achieve harmonious order, I simply needed to listen to the cube's intrinsic design principles. I burst from my room, seeking out my father to share this grand epiphany.

"Dad! I need to meet Ernő Rubik himself!" I blurted out breathlessly.

He regarded me with an arched brow. "The guy who invented that puzzle cube? Isn't he dead by now?"

"No, no!" I insisted. "He's very much alive at eighty years young! With modern pacemakers, he could live for decades more. Please, I must meet him!"

My father chuckled and shook his head. "Sure, why not? Just hop on a flight to Hungary and knock on his door saying 'Hey Ernő, it's me!' I'm certain he'll welcome you with open arms."

His sarcasm fell on deaf ears. I was determined to solve this cube and enshrine it as a life accomplishment.

"Dad! You have to take me to Budapest immediately!"

"You can't be serious. This is all because of some plastic cube puzzle?"

"It's so much more than that!" I insisted, my words tumbling forth in a fervent torrent. "Rubik has unlocked the secrets of geometrical order from seeming chaos. His cube contains over 43 quintillion possible permutations - a profound metaphor for embracing life's infinities!"

I could see the apathy glazing over my father's eyes, so I changed tactic, appealing to the businessman within him. "Think of the potential applications, dad! If I can uncover Rubik's core design principles, we could revolutionize fields like computer science, mathematics, even classical physics!"

That piqued his interest, however faintly. Sensing an opening, I drove my point home with full melodramatic flair.

"Throughout history, the great innovators were dismissed as eccentric dreamers by the unimaginative masses. But it was their wild visions that transformed the world!" My voice escalated with conviction. "Da Vinci, Newton, Einstein – their ideas seemed preposterous at first. Yet they persisted, and their names now echo loudly through the ages!"

By now, my father's poker face had eroded into restrained bemusement. I seized my advantage, doubling down on the epochal significance of this humble children's toy.

"Just think...encountering the dimensions of Rubik's Cube at such a pivotal age could be the catalyst that propels me down the path of true greatness!" I proclaimed with youthful hubris. "Like the visionaries before me, I may one day etch my own name into humanity's pantheon of pioneering geniuses!"

"You brilliant, melodramatic fool," he chuckled, ruffling my hair affectionately.

"Very well, I'll make the travel arrangements, but you must find a way to connect with him. If meeting your beloved cubist mentor is what it takes to set you on your grand destiny, so be it!"

At long last, I would drink from the fount of Rubik's transcendental geometry! The saga of my "world-changing" Rubik's Cube obsession had only just begun.

The day of our meeting arrived, and I bounded down the street sporting a rainbow t-shirt and white jeans that admittedly garnered me more giggling glances than I expected, particularly from the local men. My father kept an awkward distance, clearly embarrassed by my eclectic fashion sense.

I had succeeded in finding out where Erno Rubik would be. It was providential that he was to attend a book reading session. As we entered the conference room, the author looked every bit the eccentric genius - clad in a groovy 1970s sweater, an irreverent Louis Vuitton scarf knotted about his neck. He greeted the audience in rapid-fire Hungarian before launching into an impassioned reading from his latest book "Cubed." I immediately realized two things:

First, Louis Vuitton should avoid making scarves, as Rubik's appeared to be the ugliest offender in recorded history.

Second, I could only endure about 10 minutes of his thick Hungarian accent before tuning out, his words becoming an indecipherable drone akin to a sedating medical jargon.

My father, however, seemed to revel in the authentic cultural experience, nodding along eagerly throughout the hours-long dissertation as if he miraculously understood the language... At one point, Rubik produced his iconic cube, deftly manipulating it as he spoke. To my amazement, he re-created the same white cross that had first unlocked the puzzle's secrets for me - although his moves quickly blossomed into a vibrant mosaic of colours. Interestingly, the distinct hues made no fundamental difference. As Rubik explained in English this time, our cubes represented just two of the 43,252,003,274,489,856,000 possible permutations. His wisdom struck a profound chord: "When studying from books, many simply flip to the end to find the answers. But for me, the true joy lies in the journey - in grappling with the puzzle, not the solution itself."

Rubik's words resonated deeply within me. I, too, had developed an unhealthy obsession with manifesting aesthetic perfection on the cube. It kept me awake deep into the night, twisting and contorting the rows in maddening loops. Perhaps I needed to relinquish this unrelenting desire for a singular "correct" result, and instead embrace the chaotic, metamorphic process itself. To find peace and order within the disarray. As if compelled by a higher force, I reached out and took the cube from the tray, initiating my own metamorphosis. The reading came to its conclusion, and the audience filtered out one by one until only my patient father remained in the dimming light. He ventured outside to sample the local cuisine while I stayed behind, absorbed in the cube's infinite permutations.

My father's gruff voice pulled me back to reality. "Is this what I travelled across the world for? My son playing with child's puzzles?" he laughed and said. He then thrust a plate of paprikash under my nose. "This is the REAL reason for our odyssey!" he said winking at me.

I simply smiled, cradling the re-solved cube with a newfound sense of peace and clarity. Indeed, the answers had been here all along - not in conquering the puzzle, but in surrendering to its chaotic voyage.

"Excuse me, young one. Perhaps you'd benefit from a different perspective on that puzzle."

I look up to see the kindly face of none other than Ernő Rubik himself, the legendary inventor.

"M-Mr. Rubik! I can't believe it! What an incredible honour!"

Rubik slid into the chair opposite me with a warm smile.

"The honour is mine. To witness someone grappling with my life's work...it fills me with nostalgia."

He gestured at the tangled cube between us.

"Though I must say, repeatedly turning the same faces will only lead you in circles, my friend."

I blushed, suddenly aware of my haphazard technique. Rubik gently took the cube, studying it intently.

"You see, the true beauty lies in understanding the relationships between the rows and columns. Each turn impacts the others in intricate ways."

With deft movements, he executed a sequence I could barely follow - a row spin here, a column rotation there. The colours gradually began aligning.

"Incredible! Even after all these decades, the algorithms come naturally to you."

Rubik nodded wistfully, still manipulating the cube.

"Muscle memory becomes encoded after tens of thousands of repetitions. But do not think I solved this puzzle through memorization alone."

He looked me in the eye, his gaze intense.

"True mastery requires intuition, my friend. An innate sense of how the pieces interrelate, how each twist nudges you closer to harmony."

Abruptly, he stopped turning, holding up the half-solved cube with a sly grin.

"Why don't you try finishing it off? Trust your instincts on the remaining moves."

Nervously, I took the cube, analysing the pattern he'd established. With Rubik's penetrating gaze fixed upon me, I felt the weight of his legacy pressing down like a cosmic force. I launched into the well-rehearsed algorithm, spinning the top row a full 180 degrees with two deft clockwise rotations. Rr'. I remember seeing this notation on the Indian guy's YouTube video. My dad was onto something. The iconic clicking and shuffling of interlocking plastic pieces filled the tense silence like the workings of an esoteric clockwork mechanism. Not breaking focus, I immediately transitioned into the next sequence - a single upwards shift of the rightmost vertical column. Keeping my motions precise yet fluid, I capped it off by repeating the initial 180-degree twist of the top row. Rr'UD'Rr', Rubik whispered.

My heart pounded as the last tile twisted perfectly into alignment with its chromatic kin, forging an immaculate unified row amongst the surrounding turbulence of colours. A small victory, but one achieved through meticulous calculation rather than blind luck.

Rubik's face remained inscrutable, giving no visible reaction to my deft manipulation of his cubic masterwork. Undeterred, I pressed forward, mind cycling through the memorized lexicon of manoeuvres required to incrementally resolve the chromatic discordance.

Smoothly executing the Ru'L'ULU'F' algorithm, I shifted my focus to aligning the adjacent row, dexterously shuffling the tiles like a dynamic combinatorial gambit.

My motions gradually built momentum, settling into a state of profound muscle- memory trance as I weaved the patterns through alternating F'LF and RUR'U', also called sexy-move.

Faster and faster, I cycled through the algorithms, intuition blending with discipline as the patterns blurred into a vortex, coalescing with profound precipitousness. The final keystrokes manifested in a blindingly fluid blur: RUR'U'R'FRF'.

"I... I think I'm starting to see it!"

For the next few intense minutes, we're both silent, the only sounds the soft clicks of the turning cube. Slowly but surely, I unravelled Rubik's creation, applying his subtle guidance.

At last, with one final twist, the cube lay before me - a vibrant mosaic, flawlessly solved. I stared at it in disbelief.

"By God, I did it! Your methods... they worked!"

Rubik lets out a wheezy chuckle, placing a gnarled hand on my shoulder.

"Of course you did. Understanding the relationships is key - whether we speak of a simple puzzle, or the profound complexities of life itself."

His eyes twinkled with that sage wisdom.

"Keep trusting your instincts, and no challenge will be insurmountable. This old man guarantees it." With a final wink and pat on the back, Ernő Rubik rose and disappeared into the streets of Budapest, leaving me alone with his iconic creation - and a new-found insight into its secrets.

My father contentedly stroked his sauce-stained moustache. "You did it, son!" he exclaimed, his eyes bright with paternal pride. "This reminds me of when I first accomplished something equally monumental - like receiving my PhD in general surgery from Cambridge Medical College. Or creating the pioneering Whipple procedure for pancreatic cancer alongside esteemed colleagues in Frankfurt."

Yes, my father was an altruist in the truest sense, selflessly cherishing my moment. I couldn't help but feel my solved Rubik's cube represented an equally transcendental personal achievement. After all, I hadn't just conquered a puzzle - I had decrypted the esoteric ciphers and sacred geometries seeded within by its brilliant Hungarian architect. If I could perceive and replicate Rubik's intricate dances of interlocking rows and columns, who could say what other skills awaited me? What other complex theorems and paradigms lay within my grasp, so long as I approached them with the same intensity?

For the Rubik's cube was no mere toy, but an ingenious study in applied mathematics and physics - subjects demanding the same painstaking precision as the rifleman's scope or the surgeon's blade. Mastering its patterns required focus and mental dexterity. Yet, even as I savoured my hard-won victory over Rubik's multi-dimensional labyrinth, an old wound resurfaced - one I had desperately tried to bury beneath years of calculated determination.

Eighth grade geometry class with the notorious Mr. Fitzgerald. His rebuking tone still sliced through me like sharpened steel as he called out our marks: "Gvalani.

Four out of twenty. Being Dr. Gvalani's son clearly doesn't help you. At this rate, you'll be repeating the semester while your friends move ahead."

The memory's sting paralyzes me, transporting me back to that moment of abject humiliation, ironically unravelled by the progress and insights gained from untangling Rubik's cube.

I was once again that sad, disappointed kid who was harshly criticized by Mr. Fitzgerald's whiplash words. His criticism felt like it was permanently branded onto my mind. One 'friend' whispered, "four? What a dumbass."

I was a shipwrecked sailor adrift in adolescent mockery. I felt like I was standing naked in front of a thousand people with a bright spotlight cast upon me.

At that moment, I desperately wished to offer some futile protest - "But Prof., I didn't complete the diagrams! I thought they weren't being graded!"

Yet the instinctive urge to self-justify withered as I knew this was my mistake. My shortcoming. A pivotal crossroads where I could either break down permanently or metabolize the pain into unbreakable resilience.

I chose the road less travelled.

The following months witnessed a metamorphosis as I clawed my way back from the abyss of academic implosion. Each sweltering afternoon, I'd disembark the bus into the empty house, seeking refuge in a rigorously structured oasis of study from 3:30 p.m. to 5:30 p.m. My notebook became a sacred tome inscribed with the rites of gravitation, harmonic motion, universal gravities, and rotational dynamics. Slowly - torturously - the principles, once abstracter than arcane hieroglyphs began unravelling into understandable sequences.

Still, hurdles lingered like ancient draconian traps. I distinctly remember grappling with the concept of banked curves, the equations eluding me like ciphers carved into indecipherable alien monoliths. In desperation, I stupefied YouTube, scouring for an accessible elucidation amid the infinite content expanse. That's when I first encountered the vivid, frenetically paced lectures of "Physics-Wallah" Alakh Pandey. Here was a teacher who seemed to revel in the absurdities of his subject matter, punctuating his lessons with satirical sketches and comedian-esque banter that bordered on performance art. He'd open each uploaded video by role calling from the comment threads:

"@demon8353? Here!

@joshvines? Here!

@darthslayer? Here!"

In one episode, Pandey had donned a whimsical ambulance costume, sketching out the weight, normal force, and friction vectors acting upon the vehicle with wild, untamed gestures. Suddenly, the formidable barrier of banked curves crumbled into common sense. For the first time, physics transcended sterile equations and theorems, morphing into a darkly whimsical dimension of human absurdities. A profound realization washed over me as I binge-watched Pandey's frenetically paced YouTube catalogue: If this mad virtual professor could upend my perception of such an imposing discipline through passion and eccentric pedagogy...perhaps the same unorthodox approach could inspire even the most stolid of academics - like the dreaded Mr. Fitzgerald himself. Might I not go and suggest to him to watch Pandey's videos and take a leaf or two from his teaching style? But with his stinging words ringing in my ears, courage failed me then.

But now that crushing failure was years behind me. Meeting the brilliant Ernő Rubik had been a transformative experience that unlocked my unique way of visualizing complex patterns and algorithms. As I finally deciphered and solved his iconic cube, it crystallized my self-belief. I wasn't a failure or an idiot after all. My mind just worked differently, in a way that could be a powerful strength when nurtured properly. Rubik's cube awakened that potential within me in a profound way. Which is why, as my father and I prepared to depart Budapest and reach Mumbai, I knew I had some unfinished business to attend to.

Squaring my shoulders, I turned to my father with a resolute look.

"Dad, there's one more place I need to go to before I can be at peace. Alone." He raised an inquisitive eyebrow but didn't argue.

My destination was all too familiar:

Mr. Jawahar Fitzgerald's geometry classroom where I had been so mercilessly humiliated years before.

The classroom was dead silent as I walked straight up to Mr. Fitzgerald. The students looked confused, wondering who I was and why I was there. Fitzgerald immediately recognized me and sneered. I could see the disdain on his face as memories of me failing his class years ago came flooding back. Instead of shrinking away like I used to, I stared him straight in the eye.

"We need to talk. About how you teach."

You could have heard a pin drop. Fitzgerald's jaw dropped, furious that a former student was questioning his methods so boldly. For a moment, I thought he might explode in rage. But then something changed in his expression. A flicker of...curiosity? Maybe even a hint of respect that I was bold enough to confront him directly. The sneer faded slightly as Fitzgerald seemed to reevaluate me. This wasn't just a student he could bully anymore. It was a person unafraid to challenge him. In that moment, I knew the power dynamics had shifted. Fitzgerald realized his usual intimidation tactics wouldn't work on me. Not anymore. This wasn't going to be teacher versus student. It was going to be a showdown between two opposing philosophies of education. And I was determined to make him rethink his methods, one way or another. Fitzgerald's frown deepened with scepticism, but I detected a glimmer of morbid curiosity flickering beneath his scowling brow. "Very well, Gvalani. But this had better not be a waste of my time with those internet celebrities you seem to idolize."

Undeterred, I ushered him into the vacant classroom 9B and fired up the projector, pulling up Pandey's canonical lesson on force motion diagrams. As the eccentric physics coach burst onto the screen in his signature ambulance costume, Fitzgerald's stern facade metamorphosed into an expression of utterly bewildered awe. "Alakh Pandey?" he murmured, more to himself than me. "He was in my class several years ago - an aimless, failing student who repeated courses three times over. And now...THREE MILLION SUBSCRIBERS?!" I could practically see the gears turning behind Fitzgerald's eyes as the absurdist lesson played out in vibrant, chaotic strokes.

Could this be the catalysing moment that transformed my cantankerous teacher's pedagogy from by-the-book drudgery to passion-infused engagement? Alas, old habits appeared to die harder than I anticipated. As the video concluded, Fitzgerald rounded on me with familiar scolding blazing in his eyes.

"What is the meaning of this inanity, Gvalani? Playing videos for kindergarteners in my time..."

His sharp tongue fired off a stinging rebuke, but I simply raised my hands in supplicating placation.

"Prof., please...help me derive the expression for a safe angle on a frictionless banked road. Demonstrate how YOU would walk me through the process." For a moment, Fitzgerald seemed almost taken aback by my deferential invitation to calmly instruct rather than criticize. With a steadying breath, the scowling mentor launched into the step-by-step derivation, his strokes filling the blank whiteboard with elegant, efficient calculations. But something seemed... amiss. His teaching carried all the hallmarks of intellectual rigor, yet none of the transcendent passion and abstractive creativity exhibited by Pandey's unorthodox tour-de-force. No visceral imagery to turn the static formulae into comprehensible scenarios. As Fitzgerald capped his derivation with a triumphant flourish, he turned with a hint of his trademark narcissism:

"There, you, see? I have no need for gimmicks and..." His words trailed off as he met my unwavering, imploring gaze.

"Prof., I wasn't trying to teach you physics itself. I know you understand it way better than I do - probably even better than Alakh. What I was really trying to do was show you a different way to teach it."

There was an intense silence as my words hung in the air. Prof. Fitzgerald stared at me, his expression unreadable. For a moment, I thought he might explode in anger at my audacity.

Then he spoke, his voice low but firm. "You think you can teach me how to teach, Gvalani? I've been an educator for over 30 years. What makes you think a smart-aleck student like you knows better?"

I held his gaze, trying not to falter. "With all due respect Prof., I'm not saying I know more than you. But I've seen how engaging Alakh's approach is, even for difficult concepts. Maybe applying some of those methods could help students understand better."

Prof. Fitzgerald's jaw clenched, like he was biting back a retort. We stared at each other; the tension thick.

Finally, he gave a slow nod. "All right, I'm listening. Show me what you think I should do differently." His tone was grudging, but he was willing to hear me out at least. In hindsight I realize how gracious he was in giving me a patient hearing considering our not-so-friendly past.

I exhaled, feeling like I'd just crossed a major hurdle. Carefully, I began outlining some ideas....

I took a steadying breath before continuing. "Well Prof., for one, Alakh uses simple analogies and humorous examples to explain abstract concepts. Like dressing up as an ambulance to illustrate the forces on a moving vehicle. Instead of just stating the formulas, he acts them out in a memorable way."

Prof. Fitzgerald's expression remained stony, but I forged ahead.

"And he really engages with his audience, calling out to them by name, cracking jokes. It creates more of a dialogue instead of just lecturing at students." I gestured to the whiteboard covered in Fitzgerald's precise calculations.

"Don't get me wrong, having the proper fundamentals and theorems are crucial. But making those dry equations feel more dynamic and relevant could go a long way."

The grizzled teacher's bushy eyebrows furrowed as he mulled over my propositions. For an agonizing moment, I feared I had overstepped and would be summarily dismissed. But then Fitzgerald gave a slow, begrudging nod. Our eyes met, and I saw a glimmer of self-reproach buried beneath his effusive pride.

"Engaging viewers through humorous storytelling, relating concepts to tangible visualizations..." Another reluctant nod.

"You may be onto something." Prof. Fitzgerald dragged a hand down his weathered face, suddenly appearing every bit of his years.

When he spoke again, his gruff tone took on a softer, more reflective shade: "Do you know Gvalani, in my day, cracking jokes or 'engaging' with students was perceived as a crippling lack of classroom decorum? The instructor's role was to remain a stoic, impenetrable orator of fact and law."

A wistful shadow ghosted across his features, perhaps recalling the childhood torment I had so recently endured under his own tutelage, but which he had wilfully ignored.

"What came across as dignified discipline was in truth...a systematic crushing of youthful spirits. Demolishing the creativity and curiosity that should be nourished, not condemned," he said in self-evaluation.

Fitzgerald's gaze grew distant, bitterly reliving personal fractures in his own psyche. "I've perpetuated a vicious cycle, arming myself with the very draconian methods that shattered my own passions as a young man. Until this pursuit of knowledge, I once adored became..." A rueful shake of his head. "A joyless slog through repetitive formula and calculation."

With surprising delicacy for his brusque demeanour, Fitzgerald erased the formulaic derivations from the whiteboard. A clean slate, awaiting its next strokes of transcendent knowledge and passion. He turned back to me, his flinty exterior finally softening into the faintest semblance of a smile.

"Well then, my renegade protégé...where do you propose we begin remaking this calcified pedagogy?"

In that moment, I realized we had traversed a vast emotional chasm together – from adversarial student and teacher to likeminded architects of a rejuvenated, more compassionate educational future. My own vision of the classroom dynamics was permanently reshaped. Solemnly, I retrieved a fresh whiteboard marker, poised to trace out the first strokes of our collaborative metamorphosis.

"From the beginning, Sir... We start...from the very beginning."

A heavy silence hung in the air, charged with unspoken realizations and retrospections. And at last, his eyes settled on me, with a weary sigh, Prof. Fitzgerald finally spoke the words that validated my deepest hopes:

"Let's do it, Gvalani."

# Chapter 3

# STARRY NIGHT

Jawahar Fitzgerald and I ended up having a long conversation that day, discussing everything from physics concepts to our recent life experiences. He told me he had started taking music classes to help manage his anger issues and was learning to play the sitar. When I asked if it was like the guitar, he explained, "Yes, the main difference is the sitar has more strings and a longer neck which creates a richer, more resonant acoustic sound than a guitar. It requires immense precision in using the correct finger positions to properly fret the right strings for the accurate duration, while also keeping time with a metronome. It's helped me develop the precision needed to maintain a steady tempo and gradually increase my speed over time."

He really emphasized how crucial precision was. I then mentioned how I had found that same focused precision to be valuable in rifle shooting competitions.

Fitzgerald seemed impressed and suggested I apply for the Indian military. I quickly shut that idea down, saying "Imagining me crawling through the mud in those camouflage pants on rainy days? Absolutely not. I can barely get out of bed before the cuckoo clock signals noon!"

I then brought up my recent meeting with Ernő Rubik, the inventor of the famous cube puzzle. Fitzgerald raised his eyebrows, probably recalling my consistently poor performance in his physics classes. He asked how I found something so academically complex to be interesting. I replied, "Through my love of finding precision. I find that restricting my focus to what's important helps shed all the unnecessary distractions. It's a concept I first learned about in the Mahabharata story of Arjuna concentrating solely on the eye of the bird when his guru Drona asked what the students saw."

Fitzgerald seemed intrigued that I had that core principle from our ancient texts. He asked where else I applied the pursuit of precision in my life. After pondering for a moment, I responded, "Aha! You know, you also teach graduate-level astrophysics, right?"

Fitzgerald confirmed, "Yes, though supposedly I don't know if I have much teaching ability when it comes to conveying concepts effectively."

His trademark bluntness shone through for a moment before he continued, "Anyway, I teach master's students principles such as the rate of star formation in the galaxy, the fraction of stars with planetary systems, the number of planets per system with potentially life-supporting environments, and so on."

He mentioned there was always excitement when picking up a new topic, like their recent research into the potential habitability of the exoplanet Kepler-1649c based on predicted atmospheric and surface conditions. Fitzgerald claimed he had even co-published findings with students in academic journals.

However, he admitted that for as daunting and limitless as the field of astrophysics could be, unveiling the unknown mysteries of the cosmos, there was one key equation that continued to elude him and his students' mastery: "The Drake Equation. We've tackled so many intricate concepts in class, yet this infamous formula involving the statistical probability of technologically advanced extraterrestrial civilizations always proved too precise to solve definitively." I was taken aback at the exchange of confidentiality that was admitted by him. Imagine, my nemesis and I were involved in a **tête-à tête** as though I was his favourite disciple and he my "Guru". Little did I know that this was merely the beginning...

Listening to his confession of The Drake Equation being his waterloo, I laughed and deliberately made light of the matter saying that I didn't realize the pop singer Drake was associated with any complex astrophysical concepts.

But Fitzgerald had clearly piqued my curiosity about this deceptively simple yet captivatingly elusive equation.

Fitzgerald could see the intrigue on my face regarding the Drake Equation and continued explaining. "Don't let the name fool you. This has nothing to do with the musician. The Drake Equation is a profound attempt by scientists to calculate the potential number of active, communicative extra-terrestrial civilizations in our galaxy."

He outlined the various factors that went into the famous formula: "It considers the rate of star formation, the fraction that have planets, the number of those planets situated in the habitable zones of their systems, the likelihood of life actually arising on those worlds, and then the subsequent chances of that life evolving into an intelligent civilization capable of developing detectable technologies."

Fitzgerald shook his head, a hint of frustrated awe in his voice.

"Each of those variables requires extensive research across multiple disciplines - astronomy, physics, chemistry, biology, you name it. Accurately quantifying any one of them is an immense academic challenge in itself."

He looked at me solemnly. "Yet the greatest minds in astrophysics have spent decades calculating and re-calculating the Drake Equation, only to be thwarted by the sheer astronomical improbability and statistical uncertainties involved. It's Mount Everest of cosmic riddles."

I could feel the fever taking hold, my mind already racing with possibilities.

"But...what if someone could solve it? Definitively calculate each variable to achieve an exact statistical answer?" I asked, trying and failing to mask my eagerness. Fitzgerald gave a wizened smile, recognizing the obsessive spark he had awakened.

"Well then, my "precision" driven former student... they would be the first to quantify one of the most elusive questions plaguing humanity's celestial pursuits."

His eyes took on a distant, reverent look. "To mathematically confirm the likelihood of intelligent life existing beyond our pale blue dot...or, perhaps more profoundly, to quantify with statistical finality that we are entirely alone in this cold, yawning cosmos."

I felt myself leaning forward, utterly transfixed. My heart was pounding, an all- consuming fire igniting within my very core. This was it - the quintessential obsession that could cement my pursuit of precision into the annals of history itself.

I could barely contain the excitement as I leaned forward, eyes blazing with transcendent fervour. Fitzgerald's words had awoken a primordial hunger – the rigor mortis of my mind was shattered as hints of my true, rapacious potential strained to emerge against the corporeal shackles.

"Prof...." My voice rumbled forth, razor-edged with feverish intensity. "This Drake Equation...I don't just want to tackle its variables. I need to conquer them utterly."

Fitzgerald cocked an intrigued eyebrow, realizing he was bearing witness to the chrysalis rupturing. The erstwhile student morphing into an instinctive savant - a single-minded acolyte irrevocably bound to the path of enlightened mastery.

"You speak of astronomers failing to solve the mystery?" I stated with a rueful chuckle, "Then let them be exposed as charlatans grasping fruitlessly at the void."

My fingers clenched, nails digging indentations as the cosmic fire coursed through trembling digits. I could feel entropy's elemental chaos beginning to be unravelled and solved. "Grant me the chance to deconstruct each of the accursed equation's unknowns..." A terse inhalation, eyes blazing into Fitzgerald's soul. "And you shall bear witness as I do that I will achieve far more than mere precision."

The force of my gaze unblinkingly locked upon his. "I will reach into the abyssal tapestry of space-time and pluck out the cosmic answer...Send me into that infinite chasm, Prof.. For I shall emerge on the other side draped in the cold mantle of universal truth itself."

In that charged moment, master and apprentice peered through the cosmological looking glass, catching a refracted glimpse of the obsession's world-reaving trajectory. An event horizon where all accepted laws and limitations disintegrated into unflinching, unbridled brilliance.

"Then gaze into the abyss, my boy. And fear not its yawning black hole...for you have been forever altered in its cosmic image." Fitzgerald said, regarding me carefully for a long moment. Then, with a ceremonious nod of respect, he began gathering his materials. "Very well, Gvalani. Let's take the first step into the cosmic abyss together..."

"The seven factors of the Drake equation must be our seven horcruxes," he said, "each one a fragment of our goal." The realization hit me like a thunderbolt: I could achieve something more. Something nobody had ever achieved. Something flawless.

I departed Fitzgerald's office with a new fire in my belly. His words echoed in my mind, each one a spark igniting the tinder of my ambition. As I stepped out into the bustling corridor, a wave of determination washed over me. I wanted to take over the world, literally.

Space artifacts have fascinated me since I was seven years old. I remembered those nights, perched on a makeshift tripod with a cardboard tube, gazing into the vast expanse of the universe. The moon's craters, so like the potholes on my school road, seemed close enough to touch. One night,

I spotted a star twinkling blue. Intrigued, I squinted hard, trying to discern its secrets.

Suddenly, my vision went black. My mother had placed her hand over the other end of the tube. "Sid, stop this procrastination and go out for a run," she chided.

"But Mom, I wait all day for it to be dark. Come look, the star is blue!" I pleaded.

"Colour-blinded fool," she muttered. My mother, ever the sceptic, didn't believe me.

She didn't believe in science. She was always sporty, funny enough. Although she never made it big in track sports, she passed on her dreams to me. I, however, found solace in the laziest sport I could think of: rifle shooting.

It required something most youngsters my age didn't necessarily have, something I wished to excel at always: focus, exactness, and yes, precision. The universe, too, is a marvel of accuracy. For instance, the solar eclipse is a cosmic coincidence, happening due to the clear-cut distances and sizes of the Earth, Sun, and Moon. Even a slight variation in the Moon's size or position would prevent it.

Years later, as I revisited the memory of that blue star that I had seen along with my brother. The camaraderie that we had shared made me so nostalgic. I yearned to see the same blue star again. The naked eye was no match for the night sky's mysteries. Perhaps the telescope I had built when I was ten, along with my 20 something year old brother was still around. "Mom, have you seen my telescope?" I called out.

"Sid's telescope? We don't have a telescope. Who do you think you are, James Webb?" she replied, her tone teasing.

"No, Mom. The telescope I built with Akash when I was ten. The one we made out of cardboard."

"It's been 9 years, Sid. Surely, it's been thrown away," she said. But she disappeared into the attic, emerging minutes later with a dusty shoebox labelled "scrap from the attic" - Inside lay my cardboard tube, mounted on a tripod, a relic from my childhood. I hugged my mother tightly, overcome with nostalgia and gratitude. She had kept something so childish in perfect condition for 9 long years, through two house moves. This small, simple act melted my heart.

I turned the telescope in my hands, the cardboard edges soft from wear. As I set it up, the memories came flooding back.

This was where my love for the cosmos began, where my journey had started.

Prof. Fitzgerald's words intertwined with my childhood dreams, creating a tapestry of ambition and wonder. The universe was no longer a distant enigma; it was a puzzle waiting to be solved, and I was determined to find the missing pieces. As I looked through the tube again, I knew this was just the beginning. The blue star, the Drake equation, the mysteries of space – they were all within my reach. And with each step forward, I would honour the child who first gazed into the night sky, dreaming of the stars.

I adjusted the cardboard telescope, its familiar creaks and quirks bringing a smile to my face. The night sky, vast and dark, stretched out before me like an uncharted ocean. I focused on the spot where I remembered the blue star twinkling. The anticipation was electric. My mother stood behind me, her arms crossed, watching with a mix of curiosity and indulgence.

"You really think you'll see it again?" she asked.

"I have to try, Mom," I said, my voice steady with determination. "This is where it all started for me."

She sighed but didn't leave. There was a part of her, I knew, that wanted to see the world through my eyes, even if just for a moment. I peered through the tube, the faint outlines of stars coming into view. I adjusted the focus, my hands trembling slightly. And then, there it was. The blue star.

It wasn't as vibrant as I remembered, but it was there, flickering gently against the inky backdrop.

"It's still there," I whispered, more to myself than to my mother. "The blue star."

"Let me see," she said, stepping forward. I moved aside, and she bent down to look through the telescope. Her face softened as she gazed into the cardboard tube.

"Well, I'll be…," she murmured. "It really is blue."

I smiled, the moment feeling like a small victory.

"You see, Mom? The universe has so many secrets. And I want to uncover them all." She straightened up and patted my shoulder. "Just make sure you don't forget to eat and sleep while you're at it, okay?"

I laughed. "I'll try my best."

I sprinted into my room, clutching the telescope like a precious treasure. My heart pounded with anticipation as I placed it on my study table. The soot-covered tube felt cool and familiar under my fingers as I angled it left, right, up, and down, meticulously adjusting the angle. Finally, I steadied the telescope upright. There it was, shimmering in the eyepiece—the same blue star I had seen twelve years ago.

Twelve long years had passed since that first sighting, a time filled with dreams and questions about the universe. I had read extensively about star expansion, imagining how celestial bodies grow over time. Surely, after all these years, the star would have expanded, occupying more of the telescope's view. But no, the star remained the same size, a constant amidst the flux of my life.

Perhaps in the grand cosmic calendar, twelve years is but a fleeting moment.

"Mom, come see the blue star!" I called out once again, my voice tinged with excitement and a touch of impatience.

I hoped that she would understand my eagerness in seeing it together once again. She glanced at me, her eyes softening. Peering through the telescope, her breath caught. "A tiny blue dot... twinkling," she murmured, her fascination evident.

"Why is it blue?" she asked, the question echoing a memory from my childhood.

"Mom, I asked you the same question when I was seven. You brushed it off then," I reminded her with a grin, the memory vivid in my mind. She sighed, a touch of regret in her voice. "I apologize, son. But now, I'm dying to know. What's so special about that star?" Her curiosity mirrored my own, and I resolved to decipher the colour of stars.

My cardboard telescope wouldn't suffice for such a grand quest, so, I embarked on a project that was both ambitious and exhilarating.

I gathered a large tripod, an accessory tray, slow motion controls, a counterweight, an optical tube, three telescope rings, an eyepiece, and a finder scope. My brother, who was an engineer himself, guided me and piece by piece, I began constructing a human-sized replica of the Hubble Space Telescope. Named after the astronomer Edwin Hubble, this iconic telescope which had been orbiting Earth since the 1940s at about 27,300 km/h, completing one orbit every 95 minutes.

I chose to replicate it – albeit a poorer version - because of its ability to capture visible, infrared, and ultraviolet light. I knew it would take me weeks to put it together but If I succeeded, I could finally view the star's true colour. The parts came together slowly, each piece fitting into place with a satisfying click. I wound the slow- motion control around the tube, securing the mount and counterweight in place, and fixed the finderscope on top.

Memories of my days as a rifle shooter surfaced…

The familiar act of peering through the scope at a distant target. The blue star shone through the lens, radiant and alluring, like a beacon calling out to me. I imagined the star's blue light blending with the sky on a hot sunny day, merging with the deep hues of the Pacific Ocean. It was a royal blue, rich and profound. But as I zoomed in further, the blue faded. I blinked, wondering if I was colourblind.

Suddenly, the star turned a brilliant orange, growing larger and brighter for about fifteen minutes before shrinking and disappearing altogether.

Stunned, I scrambled to find Prof. Fitzgerald, my mentor and guide in all things astronomical. "Pinch me, Prof., I just saw something surreal!" I narrated the event breathlessly, my words tumbling over each other in my excitement.

"What you witnessed is called a supernova," he explained, his eyes gleaming with excitement. "A powerful and luminous explosion marking the end of a star's life cycle. During a supernova, a massive star briefly outshines an entire galaxy before fading from view. But how did you see that with your naked eye?" he asked, incredulous.

"I saw it through the telescope I built," I said, my voice trembling with awe and pride.

"The one made from paper?" he laughed, shaking his head in disbelief.

"No, Prof.," I corrected, "I recently built a replica of the Hubble Space Telescope."

He nodded, impressed. "Do you realize how fortunate you are to witness such an event? It's a rare and remarkable occurrence." For a moment, I felt as if it were a sign from the heavens, a calling towards space exploration. "So, why was the star blue?" I asked, my curiosity piqued once more.

"Such stars do exist. An example of a blue star is Regulus, the brightest star in the Leo constellation,"

Prof. Fitzgerald explained. "In Hindi, it's known as 'Magha,' meaning mighty. Its blue colour is due to its high surface temperature, which emits blue light."

As Prof. Fitzgerald spoke, I felt a thrill of anticipation. The star I had seen was MY Regulus, shining brightly in the night sky. Its blue hue was more than just a colour; it was a signal of its immense energy and heat.

"Regulus is fascinating," Prof. Fitzgerald continued, his voice filled with passion. "It's a part of a multiple star system, with at least four stars in its group. The primary star, which you saw, is a blue-white main-sequence star, about 3.5 times the mass of our Sun. Its surface temperature exceeds 12,000 Kelvin, causing it to emit that striking blue light." I listened, enthralled, as he described how Regulus was not only a visual marvel but also a scientific wonder.

The star's rapid rotation meant it bulged at the equator, a phenomenon that made it an object of intense study for astronomers around the world.

"Prof., the Drake equation considers factors like the rate of star formation and the fraction of those stars that have planetary systems."

"Exactly. Stars like Regulus remind us of the diversity and complexity of the cosmos," Prof. Fitzgerald said. "Understanding such stars can help us refine our estimates in the Drake Equation. It's not just about finding life but understanding the environments where life could potentially exist."

That night, I set up my telescope again, this time with a clear objective. I wanted to study Regulus in detail, to learn as much as I could about this remarkable star. The eyepiece revealed the familiar blue dot, but now, with the knowledge Prof. Fitzgerald had imparted, it seemed even more magnificent. As I observed, I imagined the complex dance of the multiple star system, the interplay of gravitational forces, and the incredible energy radiating from Regulus. I sketched the star and its position in the constellation, noting down any changes and anomalies. Days turned into weeks as I continued my observations, each night revealing new facets of Regulus. I saw faint companions near the main star, their light barely visible but their presence undeniable. I tracked their orbits, calculating their distances and imagining the forces at play. One particularly clear night, I noticed something unusual: the dimming of Regulus's light. It was subtle but perceptible. I quickly noted the time and conditions, eager to understand this new phenomenon. Could it be an eclipse, a companion star passing in front of Regulus?

I consulted with Prof. the next day, presenting my findings with excitement. He examined my notes, nodding thoughtfully. "It could indeed be an eclipse," he said.

"Such events are rare but incredibly valuable for study. They can tell us about the star's companions and their orbits." As we closely observed the Regulus binary star system over several weeks, I noticed some key patterns. The two stars were orbiting each other in a stable, cyclical manner due to their gravitational pulls on one another. By mapping out their orbits and masses, I realized there were zones around the stars where the gravitational forces balanced out. These stable zones created a "goldilocks" area where planets could theoretically orbit for billions of years without getting pulled into the stars or flung out of the system entirely. The eclipses I witnessed gave me insight into the precise choreography of these orbital motions and zones. But it wasn't just about having stable orbits. The types of stars involved - one blue giant and one sunlike star - provided the right conditions for planets to form in the first place. The more massive blue star likely provided raw material that could coalesce into planets, while the sunlike companion gave the right temperatures to potentially allow life to develop on those planets.

So, the Regulus system ticked all the boxes - stable orbits where planets could exist long-term, and the right stellar environment to manufacture those planets in the first place. It was like a planetary formation factory. This directly related to the Drake Equation's $f_p$ value - the fraction of stars that host planets. For a long time, astronomers had struggled to put a number on $f_p$ because it was difficult to observe. But by spotting and characterizing systems like Regulus that are conducive to planet formation, I was helping provide evidence to better estimate $f_p$. Systems with the right conditions were likely quite common in the universe, not outliers. So rather than just guessing $f_p$, I could use Regulus as a data point to calculate a more evidence-based value for the fraction of planet-hosting stars. Prof. Fitzgerald immediately grasped the significance - my observations were unlocking one of the key unknown variables underlying our understanding of potentially life-bearing worlds in the cosmos.

The next few days was a blur of activity. Inspired by my rediscovery, I dived headfirst into my studies, poring over books and papers, running calculations, and sketching out theories. The Drake equation became my obsession. I broke it down into its seven components, each one a mystery waiting to be solved: the rate of star formation, the fraction of those stars with planetary systems, the number of planets that could potentially support life, the fraction of those planets where life actually develops, the fraction of planets with intelligent life, the fraction of civilizations that develop technology, and the length of time such civilizations can communicate. Each factor was a puzzle piece, and I was determined to fit them together. I spent hours in the library, lost in the world of equations and probabilities.

Prof. Fitzgerald became a frequent visitor to my study sessions, offering guidance and challenging my ideas. "Remember, Sid," he said one afternoon, leaning against a bookshelf, "this isn't just about finding the answers. It's about the journey. Each discovery you make, no matter how small, brings you closer to understanding the universe." His words resonated with me. The journey, I realized, was just as important as the destination. Each late-night study session, each eureka moment, each setback and breakthrough – they were all part of the grand adventure.

On a random Thursday evening, I visited Fitzgerald with a purpose. "Prof., I believe we've made significant progress in understanding the conditions on Regulus," I said, my voice trembling with a mixture of excitement and awe. "The data we've gathered, along with recent studies from other institutions, suggests the presence of both oxygen and liquid water on one of its planets." Prof. Fitzgerald leaned forward in his chair, his weathered hands gently pushing aside stacks of papers to make room for my new findings.

"That's quite a claim, Gvalani. Walk me through your reasoning. How did you arrive at these conclusions?"

I spread out the research papers on his desk, my fingers tracing the graphs and data tables.

"It starts with this study from astronomers at the University of Birmingham and MIT. They found that the planet orbiting Regulus has a significantly reduced amount of carbon dioxide in its atmosphere compared to neighbouring planets in the system.

On Earth, we know that plant life and oceanic processes play a huge role in regulating CO2. This could be a sign of similar processes on Regulus's planet."

"Interesting parallel," he murmured, his eyes scanning the papers intently.

"But correlation doesn't imply causation. What else do you have?"

"Well, Prof., remember how we observed a blockage of infrared light emitted from the star when it passed behind the planet?" I asked, pulling out our own observation logs. "At first, we thought it was just an ordinary eclipse. But look here," I pointed to a spectral analysis chart. "This pattern is consistent with the behaviour of oxygen molecules combining with each other in an atmosphere. It's eerily similar to what we see in Earth's upper atmosphere."

Prof. Fitzgerald nodded slowly; his brow furrowed in concentration. "Oxygen... the key ingredient for life as we know it. But Siddhant, oxygen can be produced by non-biological processes too. We can't jump to conclusions."

"I understand, Prof. But there's more," I continued eagerly. "We've also detected intermittent glints of sunlight reflecting off the planet's surface. It's remarkably akin what we've seen on Saturn's moon, Titan, with its hydrocarbon lakes. Those flashes can only come from liquid surfaces - and given the planet's position in the habitable zone, the most likely candidate is water."

"Liquid water," Prof. Fitzgerald breathed, a hint of wonder creeping into his voice. "The cradle of life. But how certain can we be it's not some other liquid?"

I hesitated. "We can't be 100% sure without sending a probe, Prof. But considering the other factors - the oxygen, the reduced $CO_2$ - water seems the most plausible explanation. It fits the puzzle."

Prof. Fitzgerald leaned back, his chair creaking softly. His gaze drifted to the window, where the first stars of evening were starting to peek through. "So," he said after a long pause, "potentially habitable conditions on a planet orbiting Regulus. It's extraordinary Gvalani. But I must ask - how does this help us with $f_p$, the Drake Equation variable we're trying to pin down?"

I took a deep breath, gathering my thoughts. "It's about establishing a baseline, Prof. Think about it. Regulus is just a random blue star, similar to the one I happened to spot as a child. I didn't choose it for any scientific reason. And yet, here we are, finding evidence of a potentially habitable planet. If a star I picked by sheer chance hosts such a world, imagine how many others out there might too. Sir, we're not just theorizing anymore; we have real, observable data."

"A compelling argument," he agreed, stroking his chin. "Each star with habitable planets increases the likelihood of a higher $f_p$ value. But Gvalani, to truly constrain $f_p$, we need more than just habitable conditions. We need to confirm the presence of planets themselves, across a wide range of star types."

"That's where the Doppler method comes in, Prof.!" I exclaimed, my excitement bubbling over. I grabbed my tablet and pulled up an old video. "Remember this? It's from Physics Wallah. He demonstrated how to use the Doppler shift to not only detect exoplanets but to compare their mass to Earth's, and even gauge the radioactive flux they receive compared to what Earth gets from the Sun."

Prof. Fitzgerald's eyes widened as he watched the video. "Ah, yes. Using stellar wobbles and light curve variations to detect and characterize exoplanets. A tried- and-true method in modern astronomy. Impressive, Alakh. But why the sudden recollection, Gvalani?"

"Because it's our key to nailing down $f_p$!" I said, pacing the room now. "We don't just apply this to Regulus. We use it on hundreds, maybe even thousands of stars. Every star where we detect planets, that's another data point for $f_p$. Some might have one planet, others ten. And for each, we can assess their potential habitability based on mass and stellar flux."

"A monumental task," Prof. Fitzgerald mused, but there was a glimmer of excitement in his eyes now too. "We'd need substantial telescope time, a dedicated team for data analysis..."

"But if we succeed," I interjected, "we'll have the most comprehensive, empirically derived estimate of $f_p$ ever. It wouldn't just be guesswork or extrapolation anymore. We'd have real numbers, a genuine census of our galactic neighbourhood."

"And that," Prof. Fitzgerald said slowly, realization dawning on his face, "would revolutionize our understanding of the Drake Equation. Of life's potential in the universe. Good lord, Gvalani. Do you realize what you're proposing here?"

"I do, Prof.," I said softly, my earlier frenetic energy settling into a deep, steady resolve. "And to think, it all started with that random blue star I saw explode some time ago. Without witnessing that supernova, I might never have looked deeper into Regulus, never embarked on this journey. One chance observation has led us to the brink of redefining humanity's place in the cosmos."

We set up our equipment to monitor Regulus, focusing on the precise measurements of its light spectrum. Each night, we meticulously recorded the data, tracking the minute shifts in the star's light caused by the gravitational pull of its orbiting planets. The work was tedious, but the potential rewards kept us motivated. After several months of observations, we had gathered enough data to start our analysis. We sat down in the observatory, the night sky twinkling above us, and began the calculations.

"Okay," I said, inputting the data into our software. "Let's see what we have."

The software processed the information, displaying graphs and figures on the screen. We watched as it mapped out the orbits of several planets around Regulus, indicating their masses and distances from the star.

"Look at this," I said, pointing to the screen. "We have three planets in the habitable zone. Their masses are comparable to Earth's, and the flux they receive is like what Earth gets from the Sun."

Prof. Fitzgerald leaned in, examining the data closely. "Remarkable. This suggests that these planets could potentially support life." I nodded, feeling a surge of pride and excitement. "Based on these findings, we can estimate $f_p$ for the Regulus system. It's a microcosm of what we might find across the galaxy."

"Indeed," Prof. Fitzgerald agreed. "So, walk me through how we arrive at this value. It's crucial we understand each step."

I took a deep breath, smiled within myself at the role reversal, and began explaining,. "First, remember that $f_p$ in the Drake Equation represents the fraction of stars that have planets. But we're refining it to mean the fraction of stars with potentially habitable planets."

"A key distinction," Prof. Fitzgerald interjected. "Not just any planets, but worlds that could cradle life."

"Exactly," I continued. "Now, in our study of a thousand stars in the galaxy's habitable zone, we detected planets around 203 of them. That's our first key number: 203 out of 1000 stars, or 20.3%, have planets."

Prof. Fitzgerald nodded, jotting down notes. "So, if we stopped here, we'd say $fp$ is about 0.2. But we're going further, considering habitability."

"Right. Out of those 203 stars with planets, 41 have at least one planet that's promisingly Earth-like. By Earth-like, we mean it gets a stellar flux within 20% of Earth's and has a mass between 0.8 and 1.5 Earth masses."

"Crucial parameters," Prof. Fitzgerald murmured. "Mass indicates it could have a similar gravity, and thus atmosphere, while the right flux suggests liquid water could exist."

I pointed to our calculations. "So, out of our original 1000 stars, 41 have potentially habitable planets. That's 41 divided by 1000, which is...""0.041,"

Prof. Fitzgerald finished. "But we're not using this as $fp$, are we? It seems too conservative."

"Exactly!" I exclaimed. "Because remember, we're defining $fp$ as the fraction of stars with habitable planets. So, the real question is: out of the stars that have planets at all, how many have habitable ones?"

Understanding dawned in Prof. Fitzgerald's eyes. "Ah, I see! So it's not 41 out of 1000, but 41 out of the 203 stars that have planets!"

"Precisely! 41 divided by 203 is approximately 0.2. In other words, about 20% of stars that have planets have at least one that's potentially habitable."

Prof. Fitzgerald sat back, a look of awe on his face. "So, our $fp$, the fraction of stars with habitable planets, is about 0.2. One in five. Gvalani, do you realize what this means?"

I nodded solemnly. "If this holds true across the galaxy, it means the universe could be far more hospitable to life than we ever imagined. We're not talking about habitable planets being rare anomalies anymore. They could be... common."

"Common," Prof. Fitzgerald repeated, the word carrying the weight of a paradigm shift. "From a blue star you spotted by chance as a child, to redefining our place in the cosmos. Your work suggests that for every five stars out there with planets, one might host a world where life could flourish."

We both turned to gaze out the observatory window, the vastness of the night sky now teeming with newfound potential.

"Well done, Gvalani. This is a significant contribution to our understanding of the cosmos and the Drake Equation. If such systems are common, then the number of planets capable of supporting life could be far greater than we previously thought."

We pored over the data together, analysing the orbital mechanics and the implications for planet formation. My observations of Regulus had provided crucial insights into the fraction of stars with planetary systems, a key variable in the Drake Equation. As I gazed up at Regulus through the telescope, I felt a profound connection to the universe. The star's blue light, once a mere curiosity, had led us to a deeper understanding of the universe's mysteries.

One night, as I lay in bed, staring at the ceiling, a thought struck me. The precision of the universe, the way everything seemed to fit together so perfectly – it was all connected. The Drake equation wasn't just a formula; it was a testament to the intricate dance of the cosmos. The same precision that allowed for solar eclipses, that guided the formation of stars and planets, was at work in every aspect of the universe. I sat up, grabbed my notebook, and began to write. Ideas flowed through me, connections I hadn't seen before coming to light. The blue star, my childhood telescope, Prof. Fitzgerald 's guidance – they were all pieces of a larger puzzle. As the sun began to rise, casting a soft glow over my room, I felt a sense of clarity. The path ahead was still long and filled with challenges, but I was ready. The fire in my belly burned brighter than ever, fuelled by the dreams of a seven-year-old boy who once gazed at the stars through a cardboard tube.

# Chapter 4

# HER

The news of our groundbreaking discovery with $f\!p$ spread like wildfire throughout Mumbai. AP High School, where I had spent my formative years, wasted no time in claiming credit for nurturing my talents. The school magazine proudly proclaimed: "AP Master and Apprentice Reach the Stars!" Of course, the principal made sure to highlight 'AP' in bold lettering. Mr. Fitzgerald and I shared a private chuckle over this. We were never fond of Mr. Rodricks. He had always struck us as a self-centred, uncaring man more focused on the school's reputation than genuine learning. "You want a higher payday? Teach grad students, not school kids," he had once scoffed at Fitzgerald, unaware that tutoring university students was Fitzgerald's primary income source.

If Rodricks ever discovered this side hustle, Fitzgerald risked getting fired—a laughable prospect given his immense talents that far exceeded AP's modest means. Nevertheless, Rodricks seemed intent on basking in whatever glory he could from our achievement. When I visited the school to collect my hard-earned diploma that summer, he cornered me with his usual bluster. "Gvalani, I taught your father too, you know," he puffed out his chest. "He found the cure for pancreatic cancer with the Whipple procedure. Didn't have a problem with AP mentioning his name in the magazine then. He knew AP made him what he was."

I had to resist rolling my eyes. My father, a brilliant surgeon, owed his success to his own brilliance. But Rodricks barrelled on, his voice dripping with false modesty, "AP is going to make you the brilliant astronomer of the future. You should be indebted to us for such a great education!" If he uttered 'AP' one more time, I might have snapped and declared myself the world's worst astronomer, just to spite the man's arrogance. Instead, I simply stated, "Prof., with all due respect, I don't wish to involve the school in this endeavour. It's a personal motivation for me."

Of course, Rodricks didn't listen. He went ahead and published the 'AP Master and Apprentice' article anyway, hoping to bask in reflected glory.

My former classmates reacted with a mix of pride and bemusement when they read it. "Dude, I'm so proud of you!" one clapped me on the back. "But how'd you get so close to Fitzy? I thought he hated you!" I chuckled at the memory of my early struggles with the brilliant but demanding professor.

"Arnav, Erno Rubik had a part to play in it," I said with a smirk, referring to the conversation I had with the Hungarian.

My old Hindi teacher, the warm and wonderful Mrs. Naidu, embraced me with a beatific smile. "Kya baat hai, mere sher!" she exclaimed, calling me her 'lion' as she always did. Her joy at my achievement was utterly pure and untainted by ego.

"I'm so glad you've left your mark on AP, just like your father."

As I looked around at the modest school grounds where I had played as a child, kicked a battered football between ramshackle buildings, something tugged at my heart. This humble place, for all its flaws and insufferable figureheads like Rodricks, had nurtured the seeds of curiosity within me. Vivek, the former prankster, was now a sombre engineer. Raziya, the shining talent in English literature, was now a reputed singer - her voice still ringing with eloquence. We had scattered in a million different directions, chasing dreams and destinies...yet here we remained, bound by the celestial thread of our AP origins.

The squeals of children at recess, their innocent laughter temporarily drowned out the whirring of my mind always consumed by calculations, star charts, and existential variables. For a fleeting moment, I was transported back to simpler times when the greatest mysteries were the funny-looking cloud formations or why the sky turned such a brilliant shade of vermilion at dusk.

Despite the accolades, my obsession with the Drake Equation continued to grow.

Solving $f_p$ was just the beginning. I was determined to uncover the remaining variables. My pursuit of precision began to consume me. Every waking moment was spent thinking about the equation, plotting the next steps, and analysing data.

A few days after the visit to my alma mater, my phone pinged with a text from Ronald. He was the rifle shooting prodigy I could never quite defeat back in our school days. "Want to come over?" he messaged. "Got something to celebrate and a surprise for you." I rolled my eyes. How I had felt inferior to that smug brat back then.

He made everything look so...effortless. Perfect scores, perfect form – the instructors doted on him relentlessly. Still, I was intrigued by the mention of a "surprise", so I agreed to meet up.

When I arrived at Ronald's upscale apartment, he greeted me with that infuriatingly casual confidence of his. We chatted for a while about old times on the firing range. He was representing India at the upcoming Commonwealth Games!

"Can't say I'm surprised," I admitted begrudgingly. "Going pro was always your destiny." I allowed myself a small grin. "Though today, I can look back and be proud that I was the one who pushed you harder than anyone else."

Ronald laughed easily. "Don't sell yourself short, mate. You were one of the few real challenges I had back then." His eyes sparked with mischief. "Which is why I wanted you to be here for the surprise."

"Speaking of which..." I said, feigning nonchalance despite my growing curiosity. "What's this big surprise then?"

"Ah, she should be here any minute," Ronald answered, that sly half-smile of his raising my hackles.

"An old friend..."

The doorbell rang, and a moment later, the most stunningly beautiful woman walked in. For a few startled seconds, I couldn't place her familiar yet breathtaking features - the dark, lustrous hair, the warm tan complexion, those mesmerizing azure eyes...And then it hit me like a bolt from the blue. Avantika. The girl I had harboured a hopeless crush on all through our days at the elite Savarkar Shooting Academy. She looked even more radiant than my adolescent daydreams. Our gazes locked, and I felt transported back in time, an awkward teen again, tongue-tied in her spellbinding presence.

"Hey Sid," she said at last, her lilting voice breaking the daze.

"H-hey Avantika," I stammered, silently cursing myself. "How's, uh, shooting going?"

She rolled her eyes good-naturedly. "Terrible. Ronald here keeps bragging about his Commonwealth selection while I can't hit three tens in a whole month."

Ronald grinned unrepentantly at the playful jab. Some things never changed.

"Oh, don't worry," I assured her with a confidence I didn't quite feel. "I was there once too. Nearly gave up the sport entirely until..." I trailed off, memories of my cosmic rebirth flashing vividly.

"Until you met your teacher and found that variable in some big mathematical equation?" Avantika finished, looking faintly impressed. "I didn't know you were such a science geek, Sid. Seeing you with that air rifle at the academy gave me a whole different vibe."

I couldn't help but chuckle at the apparent incongruity. "Guess I haven't always been hip-deep in astrophysics. It was only recently, after meeting a certain professor and getting inspired by the Rubik's Cube inventor himself, that the wonders of physics and mathematics really started to click."

Her eyes widened further at the mention of Erno Rubik's involvement in my journey. "The Rubik's Cube? Now I'm really intrigued. What else sparked your interest in the sciences?"

"Music, actually," I admitted, fondly recalling the few sessions listening to the sitar played by Prof. Fitzgerald's. "Weird connection, I know. But there's something about the meditative quality of ragas, the patterns and mathematics underlying them. It helped me achieve a sort of...single-mindedness."

Avantika's eyes fairly danced with delight. "No way! Music is my life, my sanctuary. Especially the classics like Kishore Kumar." She began singing a few lines of the immortal melody *"Jab Koi Baat Bigad Jaye."*

Without hesitation, I picked up where she left off. *"Jab koi mushkil pad jaaye, tum dena saath mera..."* We held the lingering note together, feeding off each other's energy, our voices blending in long-lost harmonic union. In that moment, I felt something stir within me, an awakening of the pure, unbridled passion that had been dampened by years of single-minded devotion to the equations.

As the vocals faded, Avantika looked at me with new appreciation. "Music is my retreat from this mundane world, my escape to heaven. I wish I could live where I was served coffee by Adele singing 'Hello', while Lionel Richie braided my hair." She sighed wistfully. "And my whole house would be made of piano keys."

"You'd have to avoid *E major* ones then," I quipped. "Those ugly sounds would get old fast."

She laughed, and in that ringing sound I heard the joyous chime of rediscovery - of a kindred spirit, a soul who understood the rapture of seeking beauty amidst the chaos of existence.

"So, oh enlightened astro-physicist," Avantika teased, "Where exactly do you seek your own transcendent beauty these days? Some ivory tower observatories?"

I grinned; the old spark rapidly rekindling. "Actually, my cosmic explorations happen closer to home."

As Ronald looked on flummoxed, Avantika and I fell into animated discussion - about sublime harmonies in the wheeling motions of galaxies, the poetry underlying celestial mechanics, the tantalizing secrets still left to uncover. Our words and thoughts blended like the forces governing an intricately choreographed orbital dance. In that moment, I felt something profound awaken within me. A connection not just to the mysteries of the cosmos, but to this remarkable, equally inquisitive soul. Our conversation flowed freely, two kindred spirits connecting over our shared loves for music, beauty, and the mysteries of the cosmos.

"So, Sid, this whole astrophysics thing," Avantika said, her eyes sparkling with curiosity. "Where did it all begin for you? I remember you being obsessed with that air rifle back at the academy."

I laughed, remembering those long hours on the shooting range. "Yeah, that was my whole world for a while. But then something happened..." I paused, collecting my thoughts. "I saw this incredible sight in the night sky - a blue star going supernova right before my eyes."

Avantika's jaw dropped. "No way! You witnessed an actual star exploding?

That's..." She shook her head in amazement. "I can't even imagine how mind- blowing that must have been."

"Avantika, it blew my mind," I admitted with a grin. "Seeing the brilliant flash, watching this tiny point of light suddenly burn brighter than I could comprehend...it was like someone flipped a switch inside me. Suddenly, music wasn't enough - I needed to understand the symphony of the stars themselves."

Avantika listened, rapt, as I recounted my journey from that fateful night – tracking down the wise old astronomer Fitzgerald, convincing him to take me under his wing despite my total lack of formal training. How I'd spent years mapping the night skies, deciphering the cryptic language of celestial mechanics.

"And that whole thing led you to this...Drake Equation?" she asked, trying out the strange phrase. "Some kind of math about finding alien life?"

I nodded excitedly. "Exactly! See, the Drake Equation basically tries to calculate the likelihood of intelligent life existing elsewhere in our galaxy. But it relies on these key variables that we could only theorize about - until now."

Her eyes widened as I laid out how my team's groundbreaking observations of that innocuous blue star had allowed us to pin down one of those elusive terms. "We were able to determine, with scientific rigor, that about one in five stars should have planets capable of developing life," I explained, barely containing my enthusiasm.

To my delight, Avantika matched my intensity, peppering me with questions about our methods and the vast implications if our estimates held true across the galaxy.

Her brilliant mind -- one I had only glimpsed in fleeting moments back at the academy -- shone brilliantly as we debated cosmological possibilities. "So, you're telling me, "She said at one point, leaning forward with eyes alight, "that based on your findings, there could be millions, if not billions, of worlds with life out there? Maybe even intelligent beings looking back at the same stars we are?"

I grinned, feeling more alive than I had in years. "Exactly. And that's just the beginning. There are so many other variables in the equation we still need to investigate - the odds of life developing intelligence, technological civilizations emerging and lasting long enough to explore the stars..."

Avantika shook her head in wonder. "Sid...this is huge. You could be the one to prove we're not alone in this cosmos."

In that moment, gazing into her shining eyes, I felt a sense of purpose and passion stirring within me - not just the cold, numerical obsession that had driven me for so long, but something warmer, richer, more vibrant. A desire to share these transcendent discoveries with someone who could truly appreciate their scope.

I invited Avantika over to my private observatory, eager to share this sanctum where I danced with the cosmos.

The light seemed to sparkle in Avantika's eyes. "I would love that," she breathed.

I couldn't wait to show her all my cool instruments and textbooks. Would she be impressed by the high-powered telescopes and my extensive library of astronomical texts? Of course, she would - any self-respecting academic would go ga-ga over such a collection. But was that really what I wanted? To simply dazzle her with my intellect and resources? A small voice inside cautioned that I might be getting ahead of myself. We had only just met, after all. Still, I couldn't deny the electric charge I felt whenever our eyes met.

Calm down, I chided myself sternly. This is exactly why I became an astronomer - to explore the celestial mysteries, not get tangled up in romantic fantasies. Avantika is a colleague, maybe even a friend someday, but certainly nothing more. I had to stay laser-focused on my work if I wanted to make any meaningful contributions to the field. And yet...what if she did feel the same spark? Would it be so bad to explore that connection, just a little? After all, even astronomers needed human bonds beyond just their research. I shook my head vigorously, scattering the distracting thoughts. Though perhaps a bit of casual flirting wouldn't hurt...

As she stepped inside, her eyes widened, taking in the array of high-tech telescopes and finely tuned instruments. "This must be so cool, watching space from the comfort of your own home," she remarked, running an admiring hand along the metal barrel of the replica telescope. I couldn't help but smile at her wonderment. "Not quite from home comforts," I corrected gently. "This setup uses a full-scale replica of the Hubble Space Telescope's optics that I constructed myself."

Avantika's jaw dropped as she regarded the massive primary mirror and its intricate mounting systems. "You built this? Sid, that's...that's incredible!"

I shrugged, trying to downplay the feat even as a surge of pride rushed through me.

"I had some good advice from a mentor. And an obsessive amount of free time." I gestured towards the eyepiece. "Would you like to take a look sometime?"

Here's a simpler way to describe her presence in the observatory:

She looked completely comfortable surrounded by all the astronomy equipment and decorations - but at the same time, she seemed almost too beautiful and special to be there. The skirt she wore reflected little bits of starlight that danced in colourful patterns on the dim walls. Her long black hair fell beautifully around her face, which looked perfect, like it was sculpted by someone who makes extremely detailed and delicate artwork. As if sensing my admiring gaze, Avantika turned, and our eyes met. Full lips curved in an impish smile, she gestured impatiently for me join her at the eyepiece. "Well? Aren't you going to show me these incredible heavenly sights you've been raving about, Professor?"

I blinked, momentarily stunned by the vision of her standing so commandingly amid my life's work. Clearing my throat, I stepped forward and began cautiously adjusting the massive telescope.

"I should warn you," I murmured, concentrated on calibrating the motors with utmost precision, "once you've seen the cosmos up close and personal through a rig like this...the universe will never look the same again."

Avantika made a scoffing sound, but I detected an undercurrent of giddy thrill.

"Pretty sure I can handle it, Sid. Don't think too highly of your little star-peeper here."

But when she finally put her eye to the finderscope and gasped, I knew I had already underestimated the sheer impact of the experience.

"Oh...oh wow..." she breathed, falling instantly silent. I remained motionless,

After what seemed an eternity, Avantika straightened and looked at me with new eyes - eyes that had glimpsed realms of beauty "You...you weren't kidding. That is..."

Words failed her, and I found myself merely nodding in solemn understanding. No words could properly capture the magic of the infinite working its spell.

As Avantika turned back to the eyepiece, surrendering herself to the tantalizing cosmic visions awaiting her entranced gaze, I felt something surrender within me as well. A letting go of something fiercely guarded - that single-minded obsession that had so long sustained me. In her presence, amid the grand shimmering dynamism of the universe I had devoted myself to coldly quantifying, while something new and infinitely warmer had awakened. Something aching to experience those breathtaking celestial visions not in stoic solitude, but in the vibrant proximity of a kindred, impassioned soul.

As I watched Avantika drinking in the cosmos like an elixir of pure transcendence, the first tentative blossoms of something tender and unknown unfolded within me. An inescapable human longing to share in these inexpressible wonders, side-by-side. Love.

Was this what it felt like? It was such a novel concept to me – a supposed distraction to be avoided, lest it divert me from my path of cosmic expedition. But now, within this sanctum of celestial art I had erected, it seemed the missing final harmonica, the vibration destined to elevate both Avantika and I into higher realms of grace and discovery. In that shimmering instant, I felt the pieces of my existence click into a new, terrifying yet exhilarating alignment. A path not of content solitude, but one where the breathtaking journey was meaningless if not shared.

Where the grandest celestial revelations became hollow if not enriched by human connection, the craving of heart for heart.

Swallowing hard, I moved to stand by Avantika's side, staring into the eyepiece of my masterpiece and allowing its visions to wash over me - but this time, with the electrifying presence beside me. As our eyes drank in the cosmos in uncanny synchrony, I understood at last that this, too, was part of my quest. Not just to define, but to share.

So many years I had devoted to slaking a thirst for cosmic understanding, each precious variable solved representing progress towards transcendent Truth. Yet here, in the silent night in the "ivory-tower observatory" crafted by my own hands, the final revelation shone brilliantly. Without connection, without sharing those precious insights soul-to-soul, even the most profound findings would ring hollow across the endless night.

"I had a lovely time, Avantika. Sharing my deepest pursuit with you has been nothing short of exhilarating."

"Oh, my pleasure. I had a lovely time too. Maybe sometimes I can show you my hobbies too." Avantika replied "I would love that." I said gently.

The night ended with a simple but fulfilling goodbye between two strangers-turned lovebirds. I certainly was right that we'd be friends for a long time. Sometimes one just knows. It's the feeling of pure intentions and utter love. I couldn't believe something like that would ever happen to me. But it did. I resorted to my textbooks after that, continuing my path to glory. The second variable I worked on was $R^*$, The average rate of star formation in the Milky Way galaxy. This variable represented the average rate at which new stars were being formed in our Milky Way galaxy. It was essentially a measure of how many new stars were "born" or created within the galaxy over a given period. Stars formed from huge clouds of gas and dust in space.

When these clouds collapsed under their own gravitational attraction, they could give birth to new stars. The rate at which this process happened across the entire Milky Way galaxy is what $R*$ represented.

I thought, firstly, watching the night sky closely wouldn't help this time. Why? Because stars were born every day, and I could not simply watch through the finder scope to see how many were exactly born or how long between two-star births. For $f_p$, I could just give a closer look at Regulus to see how the atmosphere impacts the star. I was stupid enough to think I could do the same for the rest of the variables. Now, the telescope started seeming more futile than ever before. Who would have thought? A cosmic explorer, who must explore the cosmos through textbooks and not gazing at the cosmos itself. At time of adversity, I knew I had a guru, whose shoulders I could lean on.

I once again scrambled to Mr. Fitzgerald's office room, bursting through the door without knocking. "Prof., for $R*$ should I.."

"Yes, yes, come in please," Mr. Fitzgerald interrupted, his voice laced with a hint of irritation as he looked up from the stack of papers on his desk. "But do mind your manners, young man. A simple knock would suffice."

I felt a flush of embarrassment creep up my neck as I stepped inside, closing the door behind me. I wondered why he was so cross.

"I'm sorry Prof.. Can I proceed to ask you questions about our next variable: $R*$?"

He nodded promptly.

I took a deep breath, gathering my thoughts. "Prof., from our previous discussions, I understand that R* plays a crucial role in estimating the potential for life in our galaxy. After all, the more stars are born, the greater the chances for planets to form and life to emerge."

Mr. Fitzgerald nodded, listening attentively.

"So, my first question is: how do astronomers estimate the value of R* for our

Milky Way galaxy? What are the primary methods used to measure this rate?"

He replied, "As I mentioned earlier, there are two main approaches to estimating R*: observations of infrared radiation from stellar nurseries and counting the number of young, hot stars."

He flipped through the pages until he found the relevant passage. "By mapping the distribution and intensity of infrared emission across the galaxy, we can pinpoint regions of active star formation. These dense clouds of gas and dust emit significant infrared radiation as new stars are born within them."

I nodded, following his explanation closely.

"Alternatively," Mr. Fitzgerald continued, "we can identify and catalogue the number of massive, blue-tinged stars, which have relatively short lifespans. These *stellar infants*' provide a snapshot of recent star formation, allowing us to infer the overall rate."

Considering the implications of each method, I said: "But as you mentioned, both approaches have their limitations. How do astronomers recover from the potential sources of error, such as finding dust or distance uncertainties?"

Mr. Fitzgerald's expression turned thoughtful. "You make a fair point, my boy.

Neither of those methods for measuring star formation is perfect on its own, which is why a well-rounded analysis is so important." He paused, adjusting his glasses.

"For example, we can compare the infrared observations of those dusty stellar nurseries with the locations of young star clusters. That way, we can account for any dust obscuring our view. Moreover, we must consider that star formation happens at different rates across the galaxy. Some regions, like the spiral arms, are more active birthplaces for new stars than others. If we only look at a small part of the galaxy, our estimate could be thrown off." He fixed me with a piercing gaze.

"Do you understand why it's crucial to look at multiple lines of evidence and account for potential sources of error?"

"Yes, Prof.," I replied, feeling a sense of clarity. "It's clear that getting an accurate measure of the star formation rate requires different observational techniques and theoretical models to cross-check our findings."

A faint smile played across Mr. Fitzgerald's lips. "Precisely, my boy. With diligence and attention to detail, we can piece together a reliable estimate of this key variable, taking us one step closer to unscrambling the mysteries behind the Drake equation."

"Prof., practically how should I proceed?"

"First, you must immerse yourself in the latest astronomical literature on star formation rates. Compile data from infrared surveys, young star catalogues, cluster demographics, and theoretical models. Cross-reference findings, noting any discrepancies or potential sources of error."

I nodded eagerly; my quill poised to record his instructions.

"Once you have a thorough understanding of the current state of research, you can come to me to show me your findings. However, this process will require diligence, attention to detail, and a willingness to question assumptions. Are you prepared to undertake such a rigorous endeavour?"

I straightened my posture, meeting his gaze with determination. "Yes, Prof.. I am ready to tackle this challenge head-on, no matter how arduous the path may be."

"Great. Now let me rest for a while because I have had this soaring fever for a day or two now."

"Oh, I am so sorry Prof. No wonder I riled you off when I came in without knocking. I empathize with your pain. You rest while I work on finding data on recent events on infrared radiation emitted by stars."

I left his office room quietly. I thought to myself having an enlightened mind like Prof. Fitzgerald's by my side was such a blessing. Could I have considered myself an astronomer without him? Could I be on the front page of my high school "AP magazine" without him? No. Walking down the stairs, I felt like the luckiest soul in the world.

I've always had this feeling of fortune being by my side. Born into a rich family like mine, the Gvalani's, is nothing less than hitting the lottery. Now, I consider myself even more fortunate to have met the smartest man on planet Earth and beyond: Jawahar Fitzgerald. (Yeah he was bi-religious - Hindu mother and Christian father)

I went home and straightaway started my path to finding the precise value of $R*$.

*'Energetic radiation from young, massive stars is absorbed by surrounding dust clouds and re-emitted as low-energy infrared radiation. Massive young stars emit ultraviolet radiation that heats local dust, resulting in infrared emission.'* I read.

"Local dust!!" I shouted to myself. "If I can find the presence of heated local dust in the atmosphere of a planet, there must have been some sort of infrared emission."

I sought it. I dived into the data, scouring through countless astronomical surveys and infrared readings. Nights blurred into days as I sat hunched over my desk, surrounded by books, charts, and notes. My once neatly organized room transformed into a chaotic lab, with scribbled equations and star maps plastered on every available surface. My laptop became an extension of myself as I sifted through data from various space telescopes. I cross-referenced infrared readings with star catalogues, looking for patterns and anomalies. Each promising lead was meticulously noted, and I followed every thread with relentless determination.

My finger traced along the crimson swirls of an infrared map, and I envisioned the roiling maelstroms of gas and dust collapsing under their own gravity, giving fiery birth to brilliant new furnaces in the inky blackness of space.

"Infrared radiation...the unmistakable herald of stellar nurseries, of planets coalescing from the primal disk of matter encircling these newly ignited suns."

I narrated to myself: "Massive young stars emit ultraviolet radiation, heating the local dust and causing it to re-emit energy as low-energy infrared radiation.

This dance of energy and matter is a prelude to creation—just like between Avantika and I - of small dust particles that lead to-WHAT." I stopped reading and looked up for a minute. Who did I just think of?!

At that moment, Avantika's radiant smile flashed before my mind's eye, her gentle features overshadowing the cosmic visions playing out on the maps before me. The gentle curve of her lips, her sparkling eyes – it was as if the entire universe had condensed into a single, breathtaking form. "Could her beauty be a product of the same cosmic alchemy?"

I traced an outstretched finger over her imagined visage, as if conjuring her ethereal essence from the swirling clouds of interstellar dust captured in the maps. "You are the universe's crowning achievement, Avantika – a life-bearing world spun into existence by the fires of creation itself."

With renewed vigour, I turned back to my work, the vision of Avantika's smile driving me to decipher the mysteries of stellar genesis that culminated in her existence. I tried to immerse myself deeper in the texts before me. *"Stellar formation occurs when minute dust particles collide and accumulate under gravitational attraction,"* I read aloud, hoping the terminology would realign my concentration. But the universe seemed to conspire against such efforts. *"The most famous stellar nurseries include those which birthed the bright stars Altair and Vega. It is said that even stars can fall in love..."*

I paused, rereading that last line with a raised eyebrow. Was I meant to interpret that as a sign from the cosmos itself? Just as I tried to divert my mind from Avantika, I encountered a cosmic love story between two stars crossed by fate and gravity. Perhaps it was indeed a subtle nudge from the universe that Avantika and I were destined for one another, our souls intertwined like a….twin flame.

Propelled by the possibility, I leapt from my chair and snatched up my phone, fumbling with the charger cord in my haste. With trembling fingers, I tapped out a message: "I'm just remembering you as I was reading an article on stellar formation, what's up?"

I cringed inwardly. Did I sound too desperate? Too overt in connecting her grace to the cosmic processes of creation? I overthought and added a casual "Lol" in a vain attempt at nonchalance before hitting send.

To my delight and surprise, her reply came swiftly: "Stellar formation? That sounds so cool! I wanna know more - does this occur from the collection of matter, or an explosion like a supernova from an existing star?"

As I read those words, my eyes fixed on the small screen, I marvelled at her inquisitive nature. Not only was she outwardly-or physically- captivating, but she possessed an innate curiosity, a desire to understand the marvels and mysteries that enthralled me. In that moment, I realized how arrogant and insular I had been, assuming that astrophysics could only entrance those already immersed in its esoteric depths. But Avantika's question reminded me that the call of the cosmos resonates within us all to some degree. Some, like her, simply took the initiative to indulge and understand that innate fascination. Humbled, I typed out a lengthy description explaining the nuances of stellar formation – how dense clouds of interstellar gas and dust gradually accreted under gravity, forming into a protostar that eventually ignited into a new sun. I went on to detail the cataclysmic phenomenon of supernovae, powerful explosions marking the dramatic deaths of certain massive stars.

As always, she was thoroughly impressed by my knowledge and eagerly inquisitive for more. In turn, I asked her about her own passion – when might I have the chance to witness her musical talents?

"Oh, I'm in this musical revue coming up!" she replied with her trademark effervescence. "It's a one-woman play where I play a bachelorette- singing, dancing, the works! Almost like a mini-Broadway show."

"That's so cool!" I exclaimed, genuinely in awe of her multi-faceted talents and enthusiasm. "When is it? I can't wait to be there!"

Her response was quintessential Avantika - bubbly, eager, the digital embodiment of her sparkling eyes: "September 17th, 2023! I'll be sure to get you amazing seats!"

I could scarcely contain my elation at the prospect of seeing her in her element. I had once caught her softly singing a few lines of an old Kishore Kumar hit, her melodious voice floating through an open window like an angel's call. If that brief snippet could instantly captivate me, I could hardly fathom the full extent of her talents on stage. This beautiful back-and-forth, this converging of our respective passions for music and the cosmos, felt so natural, so delightfully unforced.

In an age where fleeting attraction often masqueraded as genuine connection, my experiences with Avantika resonated with an authenticity and warmth that could only hint at something profound taking root.

As our conversation drifted to other topics, I sensed this was merely the opening prelude to what was shaping up to be an epic romance, stars aligning for two seemingly disparate souls in a cosmic ballet choreographed by the universe itself. My study of stellar formation had reawakened my appreciation for the staggering forces that could give rise to such splendid beauty, not just in newborn stars but in the kindred spirits that grace our lives. And with Avantika, I could scarcely wait for the main performance to begin.

# Chapter 5

# PLUMMET

The day had finally arrived - September 17, 2023. My heart raced with anticipation as I made my way to the NSCI dome in Worli, perched on the edge of the Arabian Sea. The salty breeze carried whispers of excitement as I approached the venue, my mind oscillating between thoughts of Avantika and the cosmic mysteries I'd been disentangling. A sea of people flowed towards the entrance, many clad in ordinary black and white attire like me. But sprinkled throughout the crowd were flashes of pink - dresses, shirts, even a few elaborately styled wigs. I wondered at the significance, filing it away as another intriguing mystery to undo.

As I entered the dome, the buzz of conversation washed over me. "So many people are here to see Avantika perform." A twinge of jealousy pricked at my heart. Did she engage with all of them as warmly, as inquisitively as she did with me? Was I truly special in her eyes?

I tried to sneak backstage, desperate for a moment to wish her luck, to see her radiant smile up close before the show. But two burly bouncers blocked my path, unmoved by my pleas. "I'm her friend," I insisted, but their stony expressions didn't waver. Defeated, I resorted to sending her a quick text, hoping my words would reach her amidst the pre-show chaos. Taking my seat - third row centre, the best in the house, chosen specially for me - I marvelled at the set before me. The stage was transformed into a whimsical bridal boutique, mannequins in frothy white gowns standing sentinel at the edges. A massive, glittering disco ball hung overhead, catching and scattering light like a thousand tiny stars. The house lights dimmed, plunging the audience into expectant darkness. The soft whisper of fabric, the click of heels on hardwood - and then, like a celestial body emerging from behind a cloud, Avantika's voice rang out clear and true:

"The hills are alive with the sound of music

With songs they have sung for a thousand years

The hills fill my heart with the sound of music

My heart wants to sing every song it hears…"

Her voice soared, filling every corner of the dome. In that moment, I felt as if I were witnessing the birth of a star, more brilliant and beautiful than any I had studied in my cosmic pursuits. As the familiar melody washed over me, I knew with certainty that my fate, like Altair's, was inexorably bound to this radiant celestial being before me.

The story unfolded - a modern twist on "The Sound of Music" set in a bridal shop. Avantika played Maria, reimagined as a free-spirited girl who brings joy and music to a stuffy, high-end boutique. Her character's warmth and creativity shone through every line, every gesture. Avantika twirled across the stage, her movements fluid and graceful.

Her reimagined Maria was a vision in a flowy, bohemian-style dress that swirled around her as she danced. Her long black hair, adorned with a simple flower crown, fanned out with each spin. As she sang, her voice rang clear and sweet, filling the theatre with warmth. Her eyes sparkled with joy, perfectly capturing Maria's free spirit and love of music. Each note seemed to come effortlessly, her pitch perfect and her tone rich with emotion.

During "The Hills Are Alive," Avantika's arms swept wide, her whole body expressing the freedom and excitement of the lyrics. She moved between the mannequins in their wedding gowns, bringing them to life with her infectious energy. In the more tender moments, like "Something Good," her voice softened, conveying vulnerability and hope. She cradled the microphone gently, her expressions so genuine it was easy to forget this was just a performance.

Throughout the show, Avantika's Maria radiated kindness and enthusiasm. Whether she was leading the other characters in a rousing rendition of "Do-Re-Mi" or quietly comforting someone during a emotional scene, she commanded the stage with her presence. Her dancing was a perfect blend of the traditional musical theatre style and more contemporary moves, adding a modern flair to the classic songs. Every step, every gesture seemed perfectly timed to the music, as if the melody flowed through her.

As I watched, I couldn't help but be mesmerized by how completely Avantika had transformed into her character, while still letting her own unique charm shine through. The spotlight blazed, illuminating her in a crisp black and white ensemble - Maria's iconic alpine dress reimagined. Against her rich brown skin and cascading ebony curls, the costume took on a new life, more striking than I'd ever seen before. The audience was transfixed, pupils dilating in the dim theatre.

Avantika's voice soared, clear as a mountain stream, while her body became a conduit for pure rhythm. She glided across the stage, tapping out intricate patterns with her feet, each movement precise yet flowing. Her arm draped gracefully over a chair as she crooned, the stage lights catching the shimmer of her lip gloss. My heart raced, imagining those lips against mine.

Suddenly, she launched into a breathtaking somersault, drawing gasps and delighted applause. The music shifted, and so did Avantika - from elegant swing to high-energy shuffle, her heels somehow defying gravity. Then, in a move that left the crowd awestruck, she dropped to the floor, spinning and freezing in impossible break-dance poses. Just when we thought we'd seen it all, Avantika seamlessly wove in elements of Bharatanatyam, her expressive hands and eyes telling stories within stories. The background dancers, talented, couldn't help but fade into the background amongst Avantika's radiant performance. As little girls in frilly skirts joined her onstage, echoing the classic Sound of Music scene, Avantika scooped up a guitar. Her fingers danced over the strings, voice rising like piano keys move left to right that seemed to shake the very foundations of the theatre. The lights went out and Avantika vanished from the stage. Everyone was quiet, wondering what would happen next. Suddenly, a bright light shone on the steps in the middle of the auditorium. There was Avantika, sitting with her guitar! It happened so fast, it seemed impossible.

I rubbed my eyes, not believing what I saw. How did she move so quickly and quietly? It was like a magic trick. Avantika played her guitar for the final time. The music was beautiful and filled the whole hall. Her eyes were closed as she played, and she had a small smile on her face.

When she finished the song, she opened her eyes and looked around at everyone. For a second, she looked right at me. I felt a shiver run through my body. I thought I saw her wink at me, but I wasn't sure. Everyone was quiet for a moment, amazed by what they'd seen. Then they all started clapping and cheering loudly. I stood up too, clapping so hard my hands hurt. I was shocked by Avantika's trick, but I also felt something more. It was like I'd seen real magic - the kind that changes you. I knew that Avantika had changed something in me, and that both excited and scared me a little. I waited outside, heart pounding, fingers hovering over my phone as I debated sending another text. An hour crawled by, each minute - a year. Just as I turned to leave, my back slouching in disappointment, I heard it -

"Sid!" Avantika's voice, slightly tired from her performance.

I spun around, delighted in her presence. Stage makeup still on, sweat on her brow, eyes bright with post-performance rush. Without thinking, I pulled her into an embrace, words tumbling out in an excited rush.

"Avantika, you were incredible! Your dancing, your voice - the way you moved from style to style, it was like watching the force of nature. And that costume! You looked so..." I trailed off, suddenly aware of how close we were, the warmth of her body against mine.

"I looked so...what, Sid?" Avantika's voice was soft, teasing, her eyes locked on mine.

My mind went blank, mouth dry as though I was under the hot sun in the Sahara dessert. My thoughts were electrocuted. Before I could stammer out a response, Avantika placed her fingers on my neck, gently pulling me closer. Her lips met mine, soft and warm, tasting faintly of cherry lip gloss. For a moment, I was too stunned to react, my body frozen in disbelief and joy. As she began to pull away, my heart sank. I grew in confidence, wrapped around her waist, drawing her back in. Our second kiss was deeper, more urgent. The world around us faded away – the bustling lobby, the chatter of departing audience members, all of it receded like a distant galaxy. In that moment, our private universe contained only the rapid beating of our hearts and the sweet, tender press of lips against lips. We both had smiles on our faces, a shared look that said so much more than words ever could.

For that instant, the rest of the world faded away, leaving just the two of us.

My masculine instincts kicked in, and I held her hand firmly, feeling the warmth of her skin against mine as our fingers intertwined naturally. The simple yet profound connection between us seemed to intensify with every step we took.

We made our way out of the auditorium – both forgetting the friends and relatives, the bustling noise of the crowd fading into a distant hum as we focused solely on each other. The streetlights cast a soft glow on us as we crossed the street to my building, our hurried steps filled with anticipation.

Boarding the elevator, an electric current seemed to pass between us, heightening the tension. She moved closer, her body brushing against mine, sending shivers down my spine. As the elevator ascended, time seemed to slow down, each floor passing by with a muted ding. The moment the doors slid open on my floor, she turned to me, her eyes locking onto mine with an intensity that made my heart race. She leaned in and kissed me again, this time with a passion that took my breath away. We hurried down the hallway, barely able to contain our excitement.

The door to my apartment swung open, and we stumbled inside, our movements hurried yet deliberate. A beautiful harmony to our synchronized souls. Our breaths mingled, creating a shared rhythm. As our noses touched, I could feel the heat of her breath against my skin, a constant reminder of our closeness. This moment, this incredible experience, meant everything to me. The connection we shared felt like a discovery in itself, a new horizon of intimacy and understanding. The way she looked at me, with eyes full of trust, made me feel invincible, as if we were the only two people in the universe. This was a profound bonding of souls, a shared journey into uncharted territory.

"Sid," she said softly, breaking the silence but not the connection. "I've always admired your passion, your drive to understand the universe. But tonight...tonight I see a different side of you."

I smiled, brushing a strand of hair from her face. "And what side is that?"

"The side that lives in the moment, that lets go of the calculations and just...feels," Avantika replied.

I remembered the climax of her performance just then... "Towards the end of your performance, the light suddenly went off and then you vanished. But a second later, you appeared in the middle of the arena on the stairs. How in the world is that possible?"

She laughed and replied, "Oh, it was a rope that pulled me from the roof. My producers were hoping to give off a teleportation effect. You know, like a supernova… in your language."

"That's funny, getting technical with me," I replied, muttering "supernova" to myself reflectively as Avantika and I lay next to each other. "Supernova… teleportation… supernova… teleportation…"

"Sid, what are you thinking?" she screamed, snapping me out of my reverie.

"Wait, Avantika, you're a genius!" I exclaimed, sitting up suddenly. My mind was racing, connecting dots I'd never seen before.

"I am?" she asked, propping herself up on one elbow and looking at me curiously.

"Yes! *R-star* isn't just about the reappearance of a star, it's about its transformation after a supernova!" I was talking fast now, excitement building.

"The value of *R-star* depends on the star's reappearance time after its explosion!"

Avantika looked puzzled. "Umm, okay..."

But I was already out of bed, scrambling to my desk where I kept my astronomy textbooks. I flipped pages frantically, scribbling calculations on a nearby notepad. "Don't you see?" I called over my shoulder. "Your 'teleportation' trick - disappearing and reappearing - it's like a metaphor for stellar evolution! The time between your vanishing and reappearing, that's the key!"

Avantika came over, peering at my scribbles. "Sid, you've lost me completely. What are you talking about?"

I turned to her, eyes shining with the thrill of discovery. "You've helped me crack a problem I've been working on for months! The *R-star* calculation - it's not just about the reappearance, it's about the transformation time!"

As I excitedly explained my breakthrough, connecting stellar physics to her performance, Avantika's expression shifted from confusion to amusement to genuine interest.

"So," she said slowly, "my little stage trick helped you solve an actual astronomical puzzle?"

I nodded vigorously. "Exactly! You've no idea how important this could be.

It might help us better understand stellar evolution and-"

Avantika cut me off with a laugh. "Slow down, Starman. How about you explain it to me over breakfast? I have a feeling this is going to take a while." I grinned, suddenly aware of how carried away I'd gotten. "Deal. But first, let me just finish these calculations..."

As I turned back to my notes, I heard Avantika chuckle behind me. Little did she know, her playful 'teleportation' had indeed transported me - right to the brink of a significant astronomical discovery. "Approximately two stars have reappeared in the last year, hence our star must have a cycle of about 365 days. Hallelujah! I must confirm this with Prof. Fitzgerald." … I spoke to myself.

Avantika looked at me with a hint of disappointment. "So, you're going to leave now?"

"I'm so sorry, Avantika, but I have to go. This is big—all thanks to you." I blurted out excitedly and sprinted towards my car parked in 'P4' of my building's lot. My mother would certainly disown me if she knew I was taking the car out at 2:30 AM, but the Nobel Prize was at stake. I sped through the quiet streets, my mind racing faster than the car. The urgency of my discovery pressed on me. I reached Prof. Fitzgerald's place and parked the car on the main road with a screeching drift. His apartment building stood silent, an island of darkness amid the sleeping city. As I approached his door, I noticed it was slightly ajar. Strange, I thought.

"Prof.? Where are you?" I called out, stepping inside. The silence was unnerving. "I hate to show up at this ungodly hour, but I have something to show you. I'm sure you'll love it. Where are you, Prof.?" I knocked on his bedroom door, which was half-open. Empty. The bed was neatly made, untouched. Strange for this time of night. My heart started to race as I moved through the apartment. The kitchen was spotless, no sign of a late-night snack. The bathroom door stood ajar, revealing only darkness within. "Prof. Fitzgerald?" My voice echoed off the walls, met only by silence.

I climbed the stairs to the roof, taking them two at a time. Surely, he'd be at the observatory, lost in the stars as he so often was. But the equipment stood untouched, the dome closed tight. Back in the apartment, I noticed his phone on the bedside table. A day's worth of notifications sat unread. Fourteen missed calls – all from me. My excited message about *R-star* to no response. "Maybe he's in the study," I muttered. But it was deserted too. The bathroom, the kitchen—every room echoed my growing unease. My mind raced with possibilities, none of them good.

As worry began to gnaw at me, I noticed a door I'd overlooked before. It was slightly ajar, a sight of darkness beyond. I approached cautiously, my hand trembling as I reached for the handle. "Prof.?" I called out one more time, pushing the door open to a loud creak, revealing a sight that made my blood run cold: Prof. Fitzgerald sat slumped at his desk, his head resting on the surface, arms hanging loosely by his sides. The room was dim, lit only by the faint glow of his computer screen. Papers covered every surface, equations scrawled on whiteboards lining the walls. I rushed to his side, shaking him gently. "Prof.! Wake up!" But there was no response. His skin felt cold to the touch. Panic surged through me. "No, no, no!" I fumbled for my phone to call for help, my hands trembling uncontrollably. The operator's voice seemed distant as I explained the situation, my words a jumbled mess of fear and urgency. The paramedics arrived quickly, their professional calm a stark contrast to my frantic state. They worked swiftly, but the look on their faces told me everything. Prof. Fitzgerald was gone!

"This can't be happening," I thought, numbness spreading through me. "He was just here. We were just talking about the stars, about R*. How could this happen?" My mind struggled to process the reality of the situation. The man who had been my mentor, my guide, was gone. The paramedics confirmed what I feared the most. I sat on the floor, head in my hands, as they left to file their reports. The apartment was silent again, the weight of loss pressing down on me. I looked around the room, at the scattered papers and star charts that now seemed so meaningless. The last few months flashed before my eyes—every in-depth conversation, every burst of laughter, every shared joy. From the triumph of finding $f\!p$ to the mutual grumbling about AP High, we had transformed each other in ways that went beyond academia. We had shared a common dream, one that now felt shattered. I remembered our last conversation, his final words to me, "Go get it," said with a grumpy resolve, weighed down by sickness.

I should have taken better care of him, asked him what medicine he needed. I grieved for a life that day—a life that had changed me, made me believe in myself. As I stared at his mortal remains, something caught my eye—a pen clutched tightly in the palm of his left hand. What was he writing? I wondered. I searched his desk and gently moved his head to reveal a yellow piece of paper underneath. The writing was erratic, almost frantic, but one phrase stood out: "Eye of the bird."

"What? What does that mean?" just as I went into questioning, I remembered the story of Arjuna and Dronacharya. How Dronacharya had asked his pupils what they saw in the forest. Arjuna's answer was clear and focused: "I see the eye of the bird." Was this a message meant for me? I had shared the same with Fitzgerald and how it had inspired me. My mind raced with questions. What was he trying to tell me in his final moments? One of the paramedics, a man named Koppikar, approached me. "Who are you to him?" he asked.

"I'm his pupil... his student," I replied, my voice barely a whisper.

"What were you doing here at this hour?" Koppikar pressed.

"I had to present him with some news. But do you know how he died?" I said, my voice breaking.

"We won't know without an autopsy," the nurse interjected, her tone professional but kind. My thoughts were a whirlwind of grief and confusion.

Koppikar asked if Prof. Fitzgerald had any family. "No," I answered, feeling the weight of those words.

I had been his only family, in a way.

Just an hour ago, I was at the highest point of my life, and now, I was sitting in an ambulance, staring at my mentor's lifeless body. The contrast was unbearable.

I didn't sense the professor's ill health all this time, at least not until it hit me with the full force of reality. I had just lost Prof. Fitzgerald. He would never know that I had found the value of $R^*$, our second 'horcrux' in the quest to solve the Drake equation.

As the ambulance sped through the deserted streets, memories of our time together flooded my mind. The way he would meticulously explain complex concepts, his rare but hearty laugh, the look of pride in his eyes whenever I made a breakthrough. These memories felt like a cruel taunt now. I thought of how delighted he would have been to know that we were one step closer to solving the equation. The thought brought a tear to my eye, which rolled down my cheek and fell onto the cold metal floor of the ambulance. I had reached Prof. Fitzgerald's apartment with a heart full of anticipation, and now I was leaving it with a heart burdened by loss. The pen in his hand and the note with "Eye of the bird" seemed to take on an almost mystical significance. He had been guiding me even in his final moments, pushing me to stay focused, to keep my eye on the goal.

The weight of the yellow paper in my pocket felt almost unbearable. I pulled it out and read the words again, trying to find some comfort, some guidance in them. I looked up at the night sky through the window of the ambulance. The stars seemed to shine a little dimmer, as if they too were grieving the loss of one of their greatest admirers.

Arriving at the hospital, the ambulance screeched to a halt, its doors swinging open with urgency. The nurse, her face etched with indifference, quickly slid the wheeled stretcher out onto the cold hospital floor. I kept pace beside them, my steps quick but heavy with concern. Together, we navigated the maze of corridors until we reached the Casualty, where a stern-faced doctor barred my entry with a gentle but firm hand on my shoulder. "You can't come in," he said softly, his eyes conveying the gravity of the situation. I nodded, reluctantly stepping back.

Outside the Casualty, I found myself in a small waiting area, the sterile smell of disinfectant mingling with the anxious silence. I sank into a plastic chair, my gaze drifting unfocused into the empty air. Thoughts raced through my mind, a jumble of memories and unanswered questions. I recalled Prof. mentioning his brother, the only family he had left. It had been in passing, almost as an afterthought during one of our late-night conversations. He rarely spoke about his personal life, but when he did, there was a palpable sense of longing and regret in his voice. His eyes would momentarily lose their usual spark, replaced by a faraway look that hinted at memories and unresolved emotions. Panchgani, a village nestled amidst serene hills, suddenly seemed more than just a place. It was a piece of Prof.'s hidden life, a part of his story that he had kept close to his chest. The name lingered in my mind, evoking images of rolling green landscapes and quaint village houses.

I realized that understanding Prof. better meant delving into his past, and meeting his brother became an almost instinctive desire. I wondered about the brother's life in Panchgani. What kind of man was he? Did he share Prof.'s quiet demeanour and thoughtful eyes? The idea of meeting him felt like uncovering a missing piece of a puzzle, one that might provide insights into Prof.'s guarded nature. The more I thought about it, the more it seemed essential to reach out to him. Prof. had been there for me in my quest, a mentor and a friend, and it felt like a duty to honour his memory by connecting with his only family. Maybe his brother held stories and memories of him that would help me understand the man who had impacted my life so profoundly. This resolve grew stronger as I planned my journey to Panchgani. Finding his brother wasn't just about delivering the news; it was about forging a connection and perhaps finding some closure for both of us.

The next morning dawned with a sense of purpose tinged with uncertainty. I resolved to make the journey to Panchgani, despite the daunting task of finding someone I knew so little about. As my car wound through narrow village lanes, I stopped occasionally to inquire about Fitzgerald. The villagers' responses were mostly blank stares or indifferent shakes of the head, until a shopkeeper's eyes lit up at the mention of "Fitzgerald? Beda Ganpatrao Gali." Following his directions, I found myself at the end of a dusty lane lined with modest bamboo-and-mud houses. Parking my shiny Subaru outside, I approached a weathered door and rapped my knuckles against it. The sound echoed faintly through the quiet street. After what seemed like an eternity, the door creaked open to reveal an elderly woman clad in a faded saree, her face etched with years of weather and wisdom. "Namaste," I greeted respectfully. "I'm looking for Mr. Fitzgerald." She regarded me with curiosity, then nodded slowly.

"Fitzgerald Saab," she repeated in Hindi, understanding dawning in her eyes. "He's fetching water from the well. Follow me." We walked behind the modest dwelling to find a frail figure struggling with a rope, hauling a bucket up from the depths.

Without hesitation, I stepped forward to lend a hand. Fitzgerald glanced up, his eyes crinkling with surprise and weariness.

"Are you Mr. Fitzgerald?" I asked, already sensing the answer.

"Yes, I am," he replied softly, his voice carrying the weight of years spent in quiet solitude.

"Nice to meet you," I said, though the gravity of the news I carried hung heavy between us. "I need to speak with you about your brother."

His brow furrowed in confusion as I guided him back to his humble home. I found myself sitting on a worn mat across from Prof. Fitzgerald's brother in the living room. The contrast between this simple dwelling and Prof. Fitzgerald's life as a respected professor was striking.

"Your brother passed away last night," I said, my voice barely above a whisper. His reaction wasn't what I expected.

There was no outburst of grief, just a quiet, "Oh," and a distant look in his eyes. "How did he die?" he asked, his voice steady.

"I'm not sure yet," I replied. "Probably stress."

"He was stressed," the brother nodded, as if confirming something he'd long suspected.

"What do you mean?" I leaned forward, eager to understand. He sighed, adjusting his ponytail in a gesture eerily similar to Prof.Fitzgerald's.

"My brother, he took his work very seriously. Too seriously, perhaps. I remember his 39th birthday - he had a heart attack from all that stress. After that, he struggled with depression, couldn't sleep without medication."

I felt a pang of guilt. Had I missed signs of Prof. Fitzgerald's struggle?

"But what was stressing him out so much?" I pressed.

"It has to be that equation," he said, shaking his head.

"What equation?" I asked, although I had a sinking feeling I knew the answer.

"Since 2007, he's been obsessed with an equation to determine the possibility of life outside Earth. Some kind of fantasy, he called it. But he couldn't let it go."

As he spoke, I realized there was so much about Prof. I didn't know. The brilliant mentor I admired had been fighting battles I never saw.

"This equation," I said, leaning forward. "Did he ever talk about it in detail?"

The brother furrowed his brow, thinking. "Not really. He was always secretive about his work. But I remember him mentioning something about technical terms like $f_p$, $f_l$, $f_i$, $R^*$ once or twice."

My heart skipped a beat. "$R^*$? Are you sure?"

He nodded. "Yes, that sounds right. But it was driving him mad, I think. He'd call at odd hours, rambling about breakthroughs and setbacks. But this was years ago. Decades ago. We're not close anymore. He chose this topic for his doctoral dissertation," Prof. Fitzgerald's brother explained calmly. "But he never finished it. The equation had seven parts, and he figured out six of them."

"He knew six of them?!?!!!" I exploded, my voice echoing off the walls of the small hut. Anger surged through me, hot and sudden. "And he never told me!"

The brother flinched at my outburst, looking bewildered.

I stood up, pacing the small room, my hands clenched into fists. "All this time... and he kept this from me?!"

"I don't wish to talk about his work," he said stonily. That response was odd – the thought crossed my mind, but I quelled the feeling.

"Do you have any idea where he might have kept this information?" I demanded; my voice sharp with frustration. "These six variables he figured out?"

The brother shook his head, shrinking back slightly. "No, I'm sorry. We haven't really spoken in ten years."

"Ten years?!" I scoffed. "What, did he keep secrets from you too? What happened?"

His face hardened. "I don't want to discuss that. I think it's time for you to leave."

I stormed out, slamming the flimsy door behind me. The anger boiled inside me as I got into my car. How could Prof. Fitzgerald have kept this from me? We were supposed to be a team. I had devoted years of my life to this research, and all along, he was sitting on this crucial information. As I sped away from Panchgani, my mind raced with questions and accusations. I felt betrayed, used.

"He used me for that last variable, didn't he?" I muttered, gripping the steering wheel so tight my knuckles turned white. The realization hit me like a punch in the gut, making me feel sick and furious all at once. Years of late nights, countless hours poring over data, all those moments I thought we were working together towards a common goal

- had it all been a lie? Was I just a tool to Prof. Fitzgerald, a means to an end?

"Damn it!" I shouted, slamming my hand against the dashboard. The pain barely registered through my anger. All this time, I thought I was his protégé, his chosen successor. But maybe I was just cheap labour, a fresh mind to throw at the problem he couldn't solve. I replayed every conversation, every shared moment of excitement over a potential breakthrough. How much had been genuine? How much had been manipulation? "Six variables," I seethed. "He had six f...... variables, and he let me start from scratch. Why? Was it some kind of sick test?"

The beautiful scenery of Panchgani flew by unnoticed as I sped down the winding road, my mind a mix of betrayal and rage. I had idolized Prof. Fitzgerald, shaped my entire life around his guidance. And now, it felt like that foundation was crumbling beneath my feet.

But beneath the anger, a new determination began to take root. I'd find those six variables. I'd crack the seventh. I'd complete the equation that had consumed Prof. Fitzgerald's life - and I'd do it without him. I'd show him, and everyone else, that I wasn't just some pawn in his space-expedition chess game. "You should have trusted me, Prof.," I growled, pushing the car faster around the curves. "You'll see. I'll finish what you started, and I'll do it better than you ever could."

The road ahead stretched out before me, as uncertain and challenging as the task that lay ahead. But I was done being in Prof. Fitzgerald's shadow. It was time to forge my own path, to reach for the stars on my own terms. I paced Prof.'s study room, where he took his last breath, my fingers running through my hair as I tried to process this information. Prof. Fitzgerald, my mentor, the man I thought I knew so well, had been sitting on this knowledge for years. Six out of seven variables - he was on the precipice of a breakthrough that could change our understanding of the universe forever. The equations on the whiteboards seemed to dance before my eyes, taking on a new meaning. Each scribble, each hastily erased notation, could be a clue to those elusive six variables.

How many times had I stood in this very room, discussing theories and hypotheses, never knowing how close we truly were? Anger flared within me, hot and raging. Why hadn't he told me? We were a team, weren't we? I had devoted years of my life to this research, sacrificed countless hours, relationships, and opportunities. And all this time, Prof. Fitzgerald had been keeping this monumental secret. But as quickly as the anger came, it was replaced by a crushing sadness.

What kind of burden must this knowledge have been? To be so close to deciphering one of the universe's greatest mysteries, yet unable to take that final step. No wonder he had struggled with depression, with sleepless nights. The weight of six variables, each one a key to understanding our place in the cosmos, must have been unbearable. I collapsed into Prof. Fitzgerald's worn leather chair, feeling the full weight of this revelation settle upon me. The room, once familiar and comforting, now felt alien. Every book, every scrap of paper, could potentially hold the clues to those six variables. And somewhere, hidden among all this, could be the key to the seventh.

As I sat there, surrounded by the remnants of Prof. Fitzgerald's life's work, a new determination began to take root. He had entrusted me with this knowledge. It was up to me now to finish what he started, to uncover those six variables and push forward to find the seventh. The magnitude of the task ahead was daunting, but exhilarating. Prof. Fitzgerald had laid the groundwork, had brought us to the edge of a cosmic revelation. Now, it was my turn to take that final leap.

# Chapter 6

# SOLITARY

I stood before Avantika's colleagues, sweat trickling down my back and dampening my shirt. My voice wavered with desperation as I pleaded, "Please, I need to see her. It's important." A tall woman with sharp features stepped forward, her eyes narrowing as she scrutinized me. Suddenly, her lips curved into a knowing smirk. "Ah, you must be the star-obsessed lover boy. We've heard all about you."

My cheeks burned with a mixture of embarrassment and surprise. The fact that Avantika had spoken about me to her friends sent a conflicting wave of emotions through me – pride, guilt, and a renewed sense of urgency.

"She lives in the blue house at the end of Maple Street," another colleague chimed in, pointing down the road. "Number 42."

I blinked, taken aback by their willingness to share such personal information. "You're just... telling me? A stranger?"

The first woman chuckled, shaking her head. "Stranger? Hardly. Avantika's been talking our ears off about you for weeks. The brilliant physicist with a penchant for stargazing."

My heart clenched. I mumbled a hasty thank you and set off towards Avantika's house, my mind reeling. She had told her friends about me, shared intimate details of our time together. I meant something to her, perhaps more than I had realized. The weight of my silence over the past days felt even heavier now.

As I approached the blue house, my palms grew sweaty. I wiped them on my jeans before pressing the doorbell, its cheerful chime a stark contrast to my tumultuous emotions. The door swung open, revealing a young woman who could have been Avantika's twin. Same almond-shaped eyes, same delicate nose – but her expression was far from welcoming. Her gaze raked over me, lips curling in obvious distaste.

"You must be Sid," she said, her tone clipped. "Avantika's inside."

Before I could respond, she turned on her heel and stalked away, leaving the door ajar. I hesitated for a moment before stepping inside, the cool air-conditioned inside was a welcome change from the sweltering heat outside. I made my way through the house, heart pounding, until I reached what I assumed was Avantika's room. The door was partially open, and I could see her sitting at a desk, bent over a book. I knocked softly. Avantika's head snapped up, her eyes widening as they met mine.

In an instant, surprise gave way to anger. She stood abruptly, her chair scraping against the floor.

"Why are you here?" she demanded, her voice sharp enough to cut glass.

I swallowed hard, struggling to find the right words. "Avantika, I—"

She cut me off, her words tumbling out in a rush of hurt and indignation.

"You never texted. After we... after everything. Not a word, Sid. For days."

"I know," I said, my voice barely above a whisper. "I'm so sorry. I never meant to hurt you. It's just... my professor, Fitzgerald... he passed away."

Avantika's expression flickered, anger momentarily giving way to shock.

"What? How?"

I sank into a nearby chair, suddenly feeling the full weight of the past few days. "Cardiac arrest. His brother said it was partly due to the stress of the equation we were working on."

"The equation?" Avantika's brow furrowed. "The one you were always talking about? Is it really that dangerous?"

I nodded, running a hand through my hair. "Apparently. His brother told me Fitzgerald had been working on it for nearly three decades. He got so far, but..."

"But not to the end," Avantika finished softly.

"Exactly. And now... I feel like I need to finish it. For him."

I looked up at her, wishing her to understand. "At first, I was angry. Furious that he'd left me with this impossible task. But now I realize how selfish that was. I need to do this for him, Avantika. I owe him that much."

Avantika's expression softened slightly, but concern still clouded her eyes.

She moved to sit on the edge of her bed, facing me. "Sid, I understand you want to honour his memory, but... that equation. Look what it did to him. You could lose yourself trying to solve it."

"I know the risks," I insisted. "But you don't understand. This isn't just about math. It's about legacy, about touching lives. Fitzgerald may not have had many friends or family, but he changed my life. He saw something in me that I didn't even see in myself. He trusted me!"

Avantika's eyes flashed with a mixture of emotion – concern, frustration, and something deeper I couldn't quite identify. "But at what cost, Sid? What if you end up like him? Spending your life chasing this equation, only to... to die from the stress and anxiety of it all? Is it really worth it?"

I leaned forward, my voice intense. "He reached six variables, Avantika. Six!

Do you know how incredible that is? He lived for this equation, and even at the end, he still had the seventh variable to strive for. That's not a wasted life. That's dedication, passion."

Confusion crossed Avantika's face. "Wait, six variables? But you told me you only had two. $Fp$ and $R*$, right?"

I hesitated, realizing my slip. "Well, yes... that was true until a few days ago.

His brother told me about the others after... after it happened."

"So your 'Prof.' lied to you?" Avantika's voice dripped with astonishment,

"Some friend he was, keeping secrets like that."

"It's not that simple," I said, feeling defensive. "I only became close to him A few months ago. We were colleagues, then friends, but... there was still so much I didn't know about him or his work."

Avantika's expression softened slightly, her natural curiosity beginning to overcome her anger. "Why do you think he didn't tell you about the other variables?"

I took a deep breath, gathering my thoughts. "I'm not sure. Maybe he was protecting me, or maybe... maybe he was waiting until I was ready. But there's something else, Avantika. During his heart failure, he sent me a message. His last words to me."

Avantika leaned forward, intrigued despite herself. "What did it say?"

"'Eye of the bird,'" I replied, watching her reaction closely.

Her brow furrowed in confusion. "Eye? What eye? Whose bird?"

I shook my head, a small smile tugging at my lips despite the gravity of the situation. "I don't know. But I think... I think it might be a clue. Something to do with the next variable, maybe. Something he wanted me to find." As our eyes met, I saw a familiar spark ignite in Avantika's gaze. The same curiosity and excitement that had drawn us together in the first place. For a moment, the tension between us seemed to dissipate, replaced by a shared sense of wonder at the mystery before us.

"It could be dangerous," Avantika said softly, but I could hear the intrigue in her voice.

"It could also be the key to unlocking something incredible," I replied.

"Something that could change the world."

Avantika was quiet for a long moment, her internal struggle visible on her face. Finally, she sighed. "I'm still angry with you, Sid. You can't just disappear like that, no matter what happened. But... I can see how much this means to you. And I'd be lying if I said I wasn't curious about this 'eye of the bird' business." I could see the hurt in her eyes, the slight quiver of her lip as she struggled to maintain her composure.

"Sid," Avantika began, her voice barely above a whisper, "I think we need to take a break."

The words hung in the air, sharp and cutting. I stared at her blankly, my mind struggling to process what she had just said. The equation, Fitzgerald's last message, the hidden variables - they all swirled in my head, competing for attention. Avantika continued, her words coming faster now, as if she'd been holding them back for too long. "Your mind is somewhere else right now. You clearly can't prioritize our relationship. It's always about the equation, the variables, the mysteries. When was the last time we had a conversation that didn't revolve around your work?"

I opened my mouth to protest, but the words died on my lips. She was right, and we both knew it. "I think about you, Avantika," I said weakly, but even as the words left my mouth, I knew they weren't enough.

She shook her head, a sad smile playing on her lips. "The difference is, Sid, I think about you more than anything else in the world. I admire your passion, your knowledge, your ambition. But what I can't stand is your obsession, your desperation. It's like you're not even here sometimes, even when we're together."

Her words hit me like a physical blow. I could see now, with painful clarity, how I had neglected her, how I had taken her presence for granted while my mind wandered among the stars and equations.

"You're right," I admitted, the words tasting bitter in my mouth. "I'm so sorry, Avantika. I never meant to make you feel less important than my work."

She nodded, acknowledging my apology but not accepting it. Not yet.

"I know you didn't mean to, Sid. But intentions only count for so much. I need more than that."

An awkward silence fell over the room. I battled through my feelings and tried to reach out to her.

"Avantika, I understand your frustration. I can see why u don't have faith in our relationship. But if I have needed someone – it is now. Give me a chance. Be there with me in this cosmic struggle of mine….."

I could see the conflict raging in her eyes, but she was noncommittal. She stretched her hand and lightly pressed my own. The weight of her hands was tinged with a hint of inspiration.

"Sid, you can do it…"

I could feel Avantika's belief in me, her conviction that I could crack the equation on my own. But the truth was, I couldn't. Not in this lifetime. Not without the hidden variables. "I appreciate your faith in me," I said softly, "but I only have two values because of Prof… And now he's gone, and I have nobody."

Avantika's eyes flashed with a mixture of frustration and concern. "Why do you need anyone, Sid? This is your journey. You started it, and you will finish it by yourself." Her words were meant to be encouraging, but they only highlighted the vast emptiness I felt without Fitzgerald's guidance. The uncertainty of the Drake equation, Fitzgerald's cryptic message, and my future with Avantika all swirled in my mind, a tangled mess of doubts and questions.

I looked at Avantika, really looked at her, perhaps for the first time in weeks. I saw the weariness in her eyes, the slight slump of her shoulders. I had done this to her, with my single-minded focus on the equation.

"You're right," I said, the words heavy with realization. "I haven't prioritized you. I've been so caught up in the equation, in trying to finish what Fitzgerald started, that I've neglected everything else. Everyone else."

Avantika's expression softened slightly, but the hurt was still there. "I know you think about me, Sid. But thinking isn't enough. I need someone who's present, who's here with me, not lost in the stars."

I nodded, feeling the weight of my choices pressing down on me. "I understand," I said, my voice barely audible. "And you deserve that. You deserve better than what I've been giving you." As I stood to leave, the realization hit me hard. This was the end of the road for us, at least for now. My heart ached, but my head was already drifting back to the hidden variables, to the complete equation, to the final step I needed to take for Fitzgerald. I paused at the door, looking back at Avantika. She sat there, beautiful and sad, a reminder of what I was losing in my pursuit of the equation.

"I do love you, Avantika," I said softly. "I'm sorry I couldn't show it the way you needed."

As I walked away, my mind was already racing, piecing together clues and possibilities. I had to find the hidden variables, had to solve the complete equation. It was what Prof. would have wanted, what he had been working towards for decades. But as I stepped out into the fading afternoon light, I couldn't shake the feeling that I had just lost something far more precious than any equation could ever be.

I raced through the documents at Prof.'s house, my fingers tracing the faded ink of equations and diagrams, hoping for a breakthrough. But as the hours ticked by, disappointment settled in my gut like a heavy stone. All the research papers I found were dated to the late 90s. How could this be? His brother had told me Fitzgerald was going crazy over the equation around his 39th birthday, years later. The timeline didn't add up, and in this pursuit, I considered the chronology of utmost importance. I leaned back in the creaky office chair, rubbing my tired eyes.

"Think, Sid," I muttered to myself. "He probably chose his doctoral dissertation topic in his mid-20s, so about 30 years ago..." The papers before me were indeed consistent with topics related to the Drake equation variables - supernova UV ray emission, dust particle collection, and more. Some even explicitly mentioned $f_p$, $f_i$, $r^*$, and other variables. It was surprising to see these terms in papers dated to his PhD studies.

But a nagging question persisted: Why hadn't he mentioned finding the actual values? Was he worried someone might steal his work and find the elusive seventh variable before him? The thought of Fitzgerald, brilliant and paranoid, hiding his true progress from the world, sent a shiver down my spine. I chuckled darkly to myself. "It's almost funny. Even if I had all his notes, I wouldn't know which of the seven variables he couldn't decipher." The apartment suddenly felt claustrophobic, the weight of unsolved mysteries pressing in from all sides. I needed a fresh perspective, someone who knew Fitzgerald before he became consumed by the equation. That's when it hit me – Vilas Sir. The senior professor at my high school who had always been ahead of Prof. Fitzgerald in everything physics related. If anyone could shed light on this puzzle, it would be him.

The next day found me striding into the familiar halls of my old high school, the scent of chalk dust and floor cleaner bringing back a flood of memories. I spotted Vilas Sir in the staffroom, his silver hair catching the fluorescent light. "Hello, Prof.!" I called out, perhaps a bit too enthusiastically. Vilas Sir looked up, recognition dawning on his face. "Ah, Siddhant! Come, sit down. How are you doing? JEE preparations in full swing, I presume?"

I settled into the chair across from Vilas. The familiar scent of chalk dust and old books filled the air, bringing back memories of countless hours spent in this very staffroom. "Actually, Prof.," I began, my voice slightly hesitant, "I've decided to focus on my research for a while. I'm pursuing Prof. Fitzgerald's work on the Drake equation." Vilas Sir's expression darkened instantly, his bushy eyebrows knit together. "Forget it, young man," he said, his voice tinged with a bitterness I'd never heard before. "That psycho couldn't finish it in 30 years. Imagine chasing a doctorate for that long." His words stung like a slap, but I pushed on, determined to make him understand. "Prof., I know you may have some ill feelings towards him, but he completed six values of the Drake equation. That's more than anyone has done before."

Vilas Sir scoffed, leaning back in his chair. The leather creaked ominously under his weight. "So, he 'almost' finished it. Some of us don't 'almost' have a PhD, you know." The insinuation hung in the air like a bad odour, making me shift uncomfortably in my seat. I took a deep breath, trying to keep my voice steady. "Prof., I just want to know where Fitzgerald might have kept his work. I want to finish what he started." Vilas's eyes softened slightly, perhaps recognizing the determination in my voice. He sighed, rubbing his temples.

"Honestly, Siddhant, you're bright, but this is PhD-level work. I suggest you get back to cracking JEE." "I hear you, Prof.," I replied, leaning forward, "but I've already cracked a couple of values myself."

"You didn't," Vilas retorted, his voice sharp. "Jawahar did. He probably did this 30 years ago. I don't even know why he's making you do all his work again."

A moment of silence stretched between us, filled with the distant sounds of students in the hallway. I could feel the weight of Vilas's disapproval pressing down on me, but I couldn't let this go. Not when I was so close. "Prof.," I said, breaking the silence, "I understand your concerns. But there's more to this than just solving an equation. Sir Fitzgerald saw something in me, something he believed could contribute to this work."

Vilas Sir leaned forward, his eyes narrowing. "And what exactly did he see, Siddhant? What makes you so special that he'd share his life's work with you?" I swallowed hard, feeling the pressure of his gaze. "I'm not sure, Prof... But I know he trusted me. He showed me things, taught me techniques that went beyond what's in any textbook." Vilas Sir's expression shifted, a mix of curiosity and scepticism crossing his face. "What kind of techniques?"

"Methods for data analysis, ways of looking at stellar phenomena that I've never seen before," I replied, growing more animated. "Prof., the work Fitzgerald was doing... it's revolutionary. It could change our understanding of the universe."

Vilas sat back, stroking his chin thoughtfully. "Siddhant, listen to me. I've known Fitzgerald for decades. He's brilliant, yes, but he's also... unstable. This equation, it consumed him. Are you sure you want to follow in those footsteps?"

I nodded, meeting his gaze steadily. "I have to, Prof... I owe it to him, and to science. This is bigger than just me or him." Vilas sighed heavily, "I can see there's no talking you out of this. But be careful, Siddhant. There are forces at play here that you might not understand."

"What do you mean, Prof.?" I asked, leaning forward eagerly.

Vilas hesitated, glancing around as if checking for eavesdroppers. "Fitzgerald's work... it attracted attention. The wrong kind of attention. People who would stop at nothing to get their hands on it.

"My heart raced at his words. "Is that why he hid his research?"

Vilas nodded grimly. "Partly. But it's also because of the implications of what he discovered... they're dangerous, Siddhant. In the wrong hands, they could be catastrophic." I felt a chill run down my spine, but also a surge of excitement.

This was bigger than I had imagined. "All the more reason to find it, Prof... To protect it." At that moment, I had to tell Vilas the real reason why I visited him.

"Prof.," I began, my voice trembling slightly with anticipation, "during his last breath, Fitzgerald wrote me a message. It said: 'Eye of the Bird.' Vilas's bushy eyebrows drew together in confusion, creating deep furrows on his forehead. "'Eye of the Bird'?" he repeated softly, almost to himself, while absently scratching his chin. His eyes seemed to look inward, searching through decades of memories.

"Eye of the Bird," he muttered again, his voice tinged with perplexity. "That's... odd. Are you sure that's exactly what he wrote?"

I nodded vigorously. "Yes, Sir I've been puzzling over it ever since. It doesn't make sense to me." Vilas leaned back in his chair, his eyes narrowing in thought.

"Did he read the Mahabharata?" I asked Vilas.

"Yes," Vilas replied, leaning forward eagerly. "He did. Why?" A spark of recognition flashed in Vilas's eyes. "Wait a minute... Eye of the bird'...It Could be a reference what Arjuna tells Dronacharya in the archery contest, isn't it?" Vilas stroked his chin thoughtfully. "Jawahar... the connection to the Mahabharata... that can't be coincidental."

"You know, Fitzgerald used to take yearly trips to Haryana. To Meerut, which is close to Hastinapur."

This new information sent a jolt of excitement through me. "Really? Did he ever say why?"

Vilas shook his head. "No, he was always very private about it. But now that you mention it, it does seem significant."

I leaned forward, my voice urgent. "Sir, do you think it would be wise for me to go there? To Hastinapur?"

Vilas considered for a moment, then nodded slowly. "It might be worth investigating. If Jawahar left any clues about his work, that could be where you'd find them." As I stepped out of the school building, the bright sunlight momentarily blinded me, as if illuminating a new path forward. Hastinapur loomed in my mind's eye - not just a small town in Meerut district, but a gateway to the past and possibly my future. The ancient capital of the Kuru kingdom, now a humble settlement, held the promise of answers I desperately sought. I found myself drawing parallels between my quest and the epic tales of the Mahabharata.

Just as the heroes of old embarked on great journeys of discovery and self- realization, I too was setting out on my own odyssey. Hastinapur might not be the celestial realm of Indra, but to me, it represented a kind of intellectual heaven – a place where the fragments of Prof.'s brilliant mind might still linger, waiting to be pieced together. As I walked home, each step felt weighted with purpose. The realization hit me like a thunderbolt - Prof.'s method wasn't just about preserving his work, it was a test. A test of worthiness, of dedication, of intellectual prowess.

He could have easily left behind a set of coordinates or a straightforward manual to his discoveries. But that wasn't Prof.'s way. No, he wanted his successor to prove themselves, to demonstrate that they possessed not just the intelligence, but the passion and perseverance to carry his legacy forward. I smiled to myself, imagining my guru crafting this elaborate puzzle. In my mind's eye, I saw him hunched over his desk, eyes twinkling with mischief and wisdom as he devised each clue. He was challenging me from beyond the grave, daring me to rise to the occasion. The difficulty of the task ahead only reinforced its importance.

Fitzgerald's work wasn't meant for just anyone - it was meant for someone who could truly appreciate and continue it. As I reached home, I felt a surge of affection and respect for my late mentor. He may never have attained the title of 'Dr. Fitzgerald' in the academic world, but in the realm of scientific pursuit and mentorship, he was nothing short of a knight. Professor Fitzgerald, I mused, a title befitting a man who had dedicated his life to unknotting the mysteries of the cosmos.

That evening, as the sun dipped below the horizon, painting the sky in hues of orange and purple, I broached the subject of my impending journey with my parents and my elder brother. We sat around the dinner table, the familiar scents of home-cooked food filling the air, creating a stark contrast to the otherworldly nature of my plans.

"Mom, Dad, Akash" I began, my voice steadier than I felt, "I need to go on a trip. To Meerut, Hastinapur." I watched as they exchanged glances, a silent conversation passing between them. I braced myself for objections, for questions I wasn't sure I could answer. But to my surprise, their faces showed not opposition, but understanding. Akash proved to be my greatest supporter. He nodded to mom and dad and clutched their hands. That one nod conveyed volumes to them. "Let him go. He needs to do this to free himself…"

"Is this about the research you've been doing?" my father asked gently. I nodded, relief washing over me.

"Yes. I think… I think he left clues there. Things I need to find to continue his research."

My mother reached across the table, squeezing my hand. "We've seen how important this is to you, beta. We may not understand all of it, but we can see your passion."

Their acceptance unleashed a flood of emotions I hadn't realized I'd been holding back. Guilt washed over me as I recalled how distant I'd been over the past months, so consumed by my work and then by grief that I'd neglected the very people who had always supported me.

"I'm sorry," I blurted out, feeling tears prick at the corners of my eyes. "I know I haven't been present lately. This work, it's just…"

"We know," my father said, his voice gentle but firm. "You're on a mission.

We've always known you were destined for great things, Sid. If this is your path, then you need to follow it."

My mother nodded in agreement. "Just promise us you'll be careful. And call us every day."

I looked at them, truly looked at them perhaps for the first time in months. I saw the grey hairs I hadn't noticed before; the lines of worry etched a little deeper around their eyes. But I also saw unwavering love and support.

"I will," I promised, my voice thick with emotion. "Thank you. For everything."

As I retreated to my room that night to pack and prepare for the journey ahead, I felt a curious mixture of excitement and trepidation. The path before me was uncertain, fraught with mysteries and potential dangers. But I also felt a sense of rightness, of stepping into a role I was meant to play. Prof. had set the stage, crafted the puzzle.

Now it was up to me to solve it. As I drifted off to sleep, my dreams were filled with ancient cities, cosmic equations, and the watchful eyes of birds, guiding me towards a destiny I was only beginning to understand.

My journey to Hastinapur, or as it's now known, Meerut, was filled with high hopes and expectations. I had come to this ancient city with one goal in mind: to uncover the secrets of the Mahabharata and understand why Prof. Jawahar Fitzgerald, made yearly pilgrimages to this place. I checked into a modest motel, my home for the next five nights. The room was small but clean, with a creaky fan that barely kept the oppressive heat at bay. But I wasn't here for comfort; I was here for knowledge.

On my first day, I decided to explore the city by rickshaw. The streets were a chaos of colours, sounds, and smells. Rickshaws and motorcycles weaved through the traffic, their horns creating a constant cacophony. Street vendors called out their wares, the aroma of spices and frying food filling the air.

At a busy intersection, I spotted a chai stall. The signal had just turned red, so I asked the rickshaw driver to stop. "Cutting chai, please," I called out to the chaiwala. As I sipped the sweet, milky tea, I decided to ask for some local advice.

"Bhai Saab, yahan dekhne ko kya hai?" I inquired in my broken Hindi. "What is there to see here?" The chaiwala's eyes lit up. "Ashtapad dekhlo," he replied enthusiastically. When I asked what that was, he assured me it was the cleanest place in Hastinapur. Intrigued, and with the rickshaw driver nodding in agreement,

I decided to give it a shot. As we approached Ashtapad, I could see tall, triangular structures in the distance. A local passerby, seeing my curiosity, explained that it was a special place, supposedly connected to the heavenly abode of Lord Shiva.

Behind the sculpture, he said, was a representation of Mount Kailash, the source of some of Asia's mightiest rivers. "This place," the local told me with reverence, "is recognized as the ultimate spiritual and historical satisfaction for every yatra participant." Confused, I asked, "What's a yatra, good man?" He smiled patiently.

"It's a path to the ultimate goal, peace. To achieve it, one must sacrifice – family, friends, love – and meditate. The only meaning of life should be the music of the flowing river and meditation." I nodded, thinking of Prof.'s fascination with meditation.

"That's interesting," I mused…

"Do you know someone called Jawahar Fitzgerald?" I asked randomly.

The local shrugged. "I've met so many people here, I may have met him, or I may not have."

Eager to get back on track, I explained, "I've come on this expedition to Hastinapur to learn more about the Mahabharata."

"Oh, you've come to the perfect place!" he exclaimed. "Bhagwan Rushabhdev, the first Tirthankara, came here. Didn't he also fight in the war?"

"You bet," I replied, though I wasn't sure if that was true. "That's fascinating.

Do you know where else I can learn about the Mahabharata?"

"Perhaps Jambudweep," he suggested.

"How exactly is it related to the Mahabharata?" I pressed.

He just smiled mysteriously. "You'll have to see it yourself."

Disappointed with Ashtapad and feeling like I hadn't learned much, I decided to visit Jambudweep. However, it turned out to be just another large, isolated temple. I felt my spirits sinking. Had I wasted my time listening to chai vendors and rickshaw drivers? I couldn't help but wonder if this villager could help me understand Prof. Fitzgerald's motives, but I was starting to doubt it. As I trudged back to my rickshaw from Jambudweep, disappointment weighed heavily on my shoulders. The sun was setting, painting the sky in hues of orange and pink, but I was too disheartened to appreciate its beauty. The rickshaw driver, sensing my mood, remained silent as we bumped along the potholed roads back to the city.

I couldn't shake the feeling that I had wasted an entire day. Ashtapad had been nothing more than a collection of triangular structures, impressive perhaps, but offering no insight into Prof. Fitzgerald's fascination with Meerut. And now Jambudweep - just another large, isolated temple. Its stone walls seemed to mock me, holding secrets I couldn't decipher. As I passed through the bustling streets, the chai vendors were still out, their calls of "Garam chai! Garam chai!" mixing with the honking of horns and the general cacophony of urban India. I winced, remembering how eagerly I had listened to their advice earlier. Had I been naive to trust the words of locals who probably saw me as nothing more than another gullible tourist? My mind wandered to Prof. yet again. What had he seen in this place that I was missing? Had he found wisdom in these temples that eluded me? Or had he, too, spent his first days here feeling lost and confused? I tried to imagine him walking these same streets, talking to the same chai vendors and rickshaw drivers. What questions had he asked? What answers had he found? The rickshaw pulled up to my motel, and I paid the driver mechanically, barely registering the transaction. As I walked through the lobby, my feet felt like lead.

The day's adventures, which had started with such promise, now felt like a series of misguided detours. The receptionist looked up as I entered, his weathered face creasing with concern as he took in my dejected posture. "Saab," he called out, "how was your day? Did you see many interesting things?"

I paused, considering how to answer. Part of me wanted to brush off his question, to retreat to my room and lick my wounds in private. But something in his genuine interest made me stop.

"Awful," I replied, the word coming out more forcefully than I intended. I saw a flicker of surprise cross the receptionist's face, and I felt a twinge of guilt. It wasn't his fault my day had been a disappointment. I sighed, then elaborated, "I wasted the day listening to rickshaw drivers, chai vendors, and locals. I didn't learn anything I came for."

As I spoke, I realized how ridiculous it sounded. Here I was, in one of the most ancient cities in India, complaining that I hadn't learned anything. But the frustration of the day had built up, and now it was spilling out.

"I came here to understand why a man I admired was so fascinated by this place. But all I've seen are old sculptures, tall mountains I can see from the comfort of my window, and temples that mean nothing to me. I've listened to stories that seem more like fairy tales than history. I feel like I'm chasing shadows, grasping at wisps of smoke that disappear as soon as I get close."

The receptionist listened patiently, nodding as I spoke. There was something comforting in his silent understanding, in the way he didn't rush to offer platitudes or dismiss my concerns. As I finished speaking, I felt a mix of embarrassment at my outburst and relief at having voiced my frustrations. I stood there, uncertain what to do next, feeling very far from home and very much out of my depth. Little did I know that this moment of despair was about to lead to a breakthrough, and that the receptionist's next words would set me on a path that would finally bring me closer to understanding Prof.'s obsession with Meerut.

The receptionist's eyes twinkled with a hint of wisdom as he leaned forward slightly. "Saab," he began, his voice gentle but filled with an unexpected authority, "Perhaps you haven't seen anything yet because you haven't known where to look."

I furrowed my brow, intrigued despite my dejection. "What do you mean?"

He smiled, the wrinkles around his eyes deepening. "Have you heard of the divine sight granted to Arjuna?"

I shook my head, and he continued, "In the Mahabharata, there is a pivotal moment when Lord Krishna bestows upon Arjuna a special vision - a 'drishti'. This allowed Arjuna to see Krishna's Vishwaroop, a form in which he could perceive the entire universe - past, present, and future." As the receptionist spoke, I felt a spark ignite within me. This was precisely the kind of information I had been seeking - a bridge between the ancient epic and the cosmic observations that had so fascinated Prof. Fitzgerald.

"This divine sight," the receptionist continued, "it's not just a story. It speaks of a deeper understanding of the universe, of perception itself."

I leaned in, my earlier frustrations forgotten. "Where can I see this divine sight?" I asked eagerly, my voice barely containing my newfound enthusiasm.

The receptionist chuckled. "You can't. Only Arjuna and Krishna could. But you could read inscriptions about it in a nearby village called Kuru."

As I thanked the receptionist and headed out to find transport to Kuru, my mind wandered back to my guru. I remembered his belief that hidden within the poetic descriptions of the divine sight were actual techniques for observing celestial objects. He thought these ancient texts contained methods of converting light and processing visual information that modern science hadn't yet discovered.

Sitting in the back of the auto-rickshaw, watching the dusty streets of Meerut roll by, I couldn't help but feel a mix of excitement and frustration. I had wasted so much time visiting places like Ashtapad and Jambudweep that didn't help me in the slightest. But now, with this new lead about the divine sight, I felt like I was finally on the right track. The auto-rickshaw sputtered and coughed as we made our way through the crowded streets. The smell of exhaust mixed with the aroma of street food, creating a uniquely Indian bouquet. As we passed by ancient buildings and modern shops side by side, I wondered at how this city seemed to exist in multiple time periods at once – much like the divine sight I was pursuing. I couldn't help but wonder: What would I find in Kuru? Would the inscriptions really hold the key to understanding Prof. Fitzgerald's fascination with Meerut? And more importantly, would they reveal some long-lost scientific knowledge that could revolutionize our understanding of the universe? As the auto-rickshaw bounced along the potholed road leading out of Meerut, I felt a renewed sense of purpose. My journey wasn't wasted after all. It had just taken an unexpected detour. And isn't that, I thought to myself, often how the most important discoveries are made?

# Chapter 7

# KRISHNA

As the sun dipped below the horizon, I found myself in the heart of Kamyakavana forest. The trees loomed tall and mysterious, their leaves rustling secrets in the gentle evening breeze. My heart raced with a mixture of excitement as I realized I was standing in the very place where ancient tales had unfolded. The forest floor was carpeted with fallen leaves that crunched softly under my feet. I squinted in the fading light, desperately searching for any sign of the inscriptions the receptionist had mentioned. But all I could see were endless trunks of trees, their bark rough and unyielding, holding no answers to my questions. As darkness fell, I knew I had to make a decision. The sensible part of me whispered that I should turn back, find my way to the safety of the city. But something deeper, an instinct I couldn't explain, urged me to stay. I thought of Prof., of his unwavering belief that this place held secrets beyond our understanding. Would he have turned back? I doubted it. So, I settled down for the night, using a large, gnarled tree root as my pillow.

The forest floor was hard and uneven beneath me, but I barely noticed the discomfort. My head was on my backpack and my mind was too full of questions, of hopes, of fears. As the last remnants of daylight faded, the forest came alive with night sounds.

Crickets chirped their nightly chorus, occasionally punctuated by the hoot of an owl or the rustle of some unseen creature moving through the underbrush. The unfamiliar noises set my nerves on edge, but I forced myself to remain still, to breathe deeply and calm my racing heart. I gazed up at the sky, visible in patches through the canopy of leaves above. The stars seemed brighter here, away from the city's lights, twinkling like diamonds scattered across a velvet cloth. As my eyes adjusted to the darkness, I found myself speaking softly, my words barely a whisper in the vast silence of the forest.

"Prof. Fitzgerald," I murmured, "if you can hear me, if you're out there somewhere... I could really use your guidance right now. Am I on the right path? What am I missing?"

The forest remained silent, offering no response to my plea.

The weight of that silence pressed down on me oppressively. I strained my ears, hoping for some sign, some whisper of wisdom carried on the night breeze. But there was nothing - just the soft rustle of leaves and the distant call of a night bird.

Seconds stretched into minutes, each moment of silence deepening my sense of isolation. The enormity of what I was trying to accomplish crashed down upon me.

Here I was, lying on the forest floor, talking to a dead man, hoping for answers that might not even exist. A lump formed in my throat, and I felt a stinging sensation behind my eyes. The folly of my quest suddenly seemed overwhelming. What was I doing here, chasing shadows and legends? Prof. was gone, and with him, perhaps, the key to understanding this place's mysteries. I let out a long, shuddering sigh, feeling the fight drain out of me. My eyes, which had been scanning the canopy above for some sign, any sign, slowly lowered. The excitement that had carried me this far ebbed away, leaving behind a hollow ache of disappointment.

"I'm sorry, Prof.," I whispered, my voice barely audible even to myself. "I thought I could follow in your footsteps, but maybe I'm just not cut out for this. Maybe I've been chasing a fool's dream all along." I closed my eyes, ready to give in to exhaustion and dejection. The cool forest air felt damp against my skin, and I shivered slightly, feeling very small and very alone in the vastness of the night. But then, just as I was about to surrender to sleep and the admission of defeat, something made me open my eyes once more. And there, streaking across the inky black sky, was a flash of light so bright and sudden it took my breath away. For a moment, I lay frozen, wondering if my desperate mind had conjured an illusion.

But then another brilliant streak appeared, and another, until the night sky was alive with falling stars. My earlier despondency evaporated, replaced by a surge of wonder and awe. I scrambled to sit up, my eyes wide and unblinking, afraid to miss even a second of this celestial spectacle. The stars seemed to dance across the heavens, some flashing by in the blink of an eye, others tracing languid arcs that lingered in my vision long after they had faded. Time lost all meaning as I watched the celestial display. It could have been minutes or hours; I couldn't tell. All I knew was that I had never seen anything so beautiful, so awe-inspiring in my life. Each new star that appeared sent a thrill through me, and I found myself holding my breath, waiting for the next one to streak across the sky. As I watched, a memory stirred in the back of my mind. Something Prof. had once said about the movement of celestial bodies, about patterns hidden in the chaos of the night sky. Could this be what he had meant? Was this spectacular display more than just a coincidence?

With each passing star, I felt a growing sense of certainty. This wasn't just a random occurrence. It was a message, a sign meant just for me. Prof. Fitzgerald had led me here, to this exact spot, on this exact night, to witness this extraordinary event. As the shower of stars began to slow, I closed my eyes and made a wish.

Not for wealth or fame or any earthly desire, but for understanding. For the wisdom to see what Fitzgerald had seen, to unravel the mysteries that had brought him back to this place year after year. When I opened my eyes again, the sky had returned to its usual stillness. But something had changed. The forest no longer felt alien. Instead, it seemed to embrace me, to welcome me as if I belonged here. A sense of peace washed over me, along with a renewed determination. I might not have found the inscriptions I was looking for, but I had seen a sight to remember for life.

As I settled back down, preparing to sleep under the watchful eyes of the stars, I smiled to myself. In this ancient forest, under this vast sky, I was finally starting to understand the mysteries that had captivated Prof. because, now; it had captivated me as well. The night air grew cooler, but I barely noticed. My mind was alive with possibilities, with questions waiting to be answered. As I drifted off to sleep, the whisper of the leaves and the distant call of a night bird merged into a lullaby, a song of secrets waiting to be uncovered. And in my dreams, I saw the stars dance once more.

The forest awakened me at dawn, the sun's bright orange glow filtering through the canopy. For a moment, I lay there, disoriented, fragments of a dream about golden stars dancing in the night sky lingering in my mind. But as my senses sharpened, I realized it wasn't a dream at all. The celestial display had been real, a memory now etched indelibly in my consciousness. I rose, stretching my stiff limbs, and set out once more on my quest to uncover insights into spirituality. The forest seemed different in the daylight, less mysterious but no less enchanting.

Birds called to one another; their melodies punctuated by the rustle of small creatures scurrying through the underbrush. As the sun climbed higher, its heat intensifying, I began to wonder if my journey would yield anything of substance.

But just as doubt started to creep in, I stumbled upon something – or rather, someone – extraordinary. There, seated on a moss-covered rock in a small clearing, was an old sage. He was a diminutive figure, no more than five feet tall, with skin weathered by years of exposure to the elements. His head was nearly bald, save for a wispy ring of white hair that circled it like a halo. A long, snowy beard flowed down his chest, moving slightly with each breath he took. At first, I thought he was asleep. His eyes were closed, and he sat so still he might have been carved from the very stone he rested upon. But as I approached, his eyes fluttered open, revealing irises as dark and deep as the night sky.

"Namaste," I said, my voice sounding unnaturally loud in the quiet of the forest. "I'm sorry to disturb you. I didn't expect to find anyone else here."

The old man's lips curved into a gentle smile. "Ah, but are we truly the only living beings here? Listen closely, young one. The forest teems with life."

As if on cue, a chorus of birdsong erupted around us, accompanied by the distant chatter of monkeys. I couldn't help but smile at the timing.

"You're right, of course," I admitted. "I'm Siddhant. I've come from Mumbai, seeking... well, I'm not entirely sure what I'm seeking, to be honest."

The old man nodded sagely. The old man's eyes narrowed slightly, a hint of impatience creeping into his weathered features. "Many come to these woods in search of something, though few can name what it is they hope to find," he said, his voice carrying a slight edge. "Tell me, young Siddhant, what brings you so far from home? And do be quick about it."

His abrupt tone caught me off guard. This wasn't the serene, infinitely patient sage I had expected to encounter in the depths of Kamyakavana. There was a sharpness to him, a no-nonsense air that demanded directness. I swallowed hard, suddenly feeling like a schoolboy called to account for some misdeed. "Well," I began, trying to gather my thoughts, "I'm here because of a promise I made to my mentor. He spent years pursuing the unknown..." I did not tell the man what exactly Fitzgerald was pursuing – knowing he would not understand it.

The old man snorted, a sound somewhere between amusement and derision.

"Hidden truths, you say? And what makes you think you're equipped to uncover them, boy? Your guru may have spent years here and apparently found nothing concrete. What do you hope to accomplish?"

His words stung, but I could sense a challenge in them. It was as if he were testing me, probing to see if I had the mettle to pursue this quest.

"Prof. passed away before he could complete his work," I explained, my voice growing stronger as I spoke. "I'm here to finish what he started. I may not have his years of experience, but I have his notes, his theories. And I have a promise to keep."

The old man's expression softened almost imperceptibly. "A promise, eh? Well, that's something, I suppose. But tell me this - do you even know what you're looking for? Or are you just stumbling about in the dark, hoping to trip over some grand revelation?"

His bluntness was oddly refreshing. It grounded our conversation in reality. I found myself responding kindly. "Honestly? I'm not entirely sure what I'm looking for," I admitted. "Prof. believed there were connections here between ancient wisdom and modern science. Something about the nature of perception, of reality itself. I'm here to understand what he saw, what drew him back year after year."

The old man leaned back, stroking his beard thoughtfully. Despite his gruff demeanour, I could see a spark of interest in his eyes. "Hmm. At least you're honest about your ignorance. That's a start, I suppose. Now, what do you know of moksha, boy? And don't give me some textbook definition - I want to know what you understand of it."

As he fixed me with his penetrating gaze, I realized that this encounter, prickly as it might be, could be the key to unscrambling the mysteries that had brought me to Kamyakavana. The old man's brusque manner might just be the steppingstone I needed to sharpen my understanding. I hesitated, unsure how to explain my quest to this stranger. But something in his worn-down eyes encouraged me to open up.

"I'm here because of a promise," I began. "A promise to a dear friend, a mentor really. Jawahar Fitzgerald. He used to make a yearly visit to Hastinapur, err Meerut. I believe there are hidden truths here, in Kamyakavana. But he passed away before he could complete his work. I'm here to finish what he started."

The old man listened intently, his dark eyes never leaving my face. When I finished, he stroked his beard thoughtfully. "Ah, I see. And tell me, what do you know of moksha?"

The repeated question caught me off guard. "Moksha? You mean salvation? I know it's important in Hinduism, but I'm afraid my understanding is limited."

The old man chuckled softly. "Many Hindus speak of moksha, but few truly understand its nature. It is not merely salvation, but the liberation of the soul from the cycle of birth and death. To achieve it, some believe one must sacrifice everything – love, family, all earthly attachments."

I frowned, considering his words. "But surely not everyone can do that? We can't all renounce the world, can we?"

He smiled, a twinkle in his eye. "Ah, you see clearly, young one. Life is not the same as it was in ages past. I have given up everything because I am a spirit, not bound by material needs. But this path is not for everyone."

As he spoke, I noticed a small wooden flute lying beside him. "Do you play?" I asked, gesturing towards the instrument.

The old man's face lit up. "Ah, yes. Music is one of the few earthly pleasures I allow myself. Would you like to hear a tune?"

I nodded eagerly, and he picked up the flute, bringing it to his lips. The melody that flowed forth was unlike anything I had ever heard – sweet and melancholic, joyous and contemplative all at once. It seemed to speak of ancient truths, of the eternal dance of creation and destruction.

When the last note faded away, we sat in silence for a moment, the music still echoing in our hearts. Clearing my throat, which suddenly felt tight with emotion, I asked, "What's your name?" As soon as the words left my mouth, I realized how mundane they sounded after the transcendent experience of the music. Yet, I felt an overwhelming need to know more about this enigmatic figure who could conjure such magic with a simple wooden flute. The question hung in the air between us, mingling with the lingering echoes of the melody. The old man's smile deepened, creasing his weathered face with a network of fine lines that spoke of a lifetime of laughter and contemplation. He seemed to be weighing his response, as if his name were a secret of great importance, not to be shared lightly.

"Krishna," he replied.

I couldn't help but laugh. "Krishna? Like the god?"

He shrugged, a mischievous smile playing on his lips. "My parents gave me this name when I was young. They said I had a habit of loving the taste of "maakhan" or butter. And, as you've seen, I do play the flute rather well."

As we talked, I found myself drawn to this enigmatic figure. His words were filled with wisdom, yet he spoke with the playfulness of a child. He seemed to embody the very spirit of the forest – ancient and ever-renewing, serious and mirthful.

"Krishna," I said, tasting the name on my tongue. "I've only just met you, but I feel like I've known you for ages. There's something familiar about you."

He nodded, his eyes twinkling. "Perhaps we have met before, in another life. Or perhaps you simply recognize a kindred spirit. Now tell me, Siddhant- a name that means 'principles,' does it not? -You care deeply for this man, this Fitzgerald. But tell me, why Kamyakavana? What answers do you believe lie here, that would draw you all the way from Mumbai?"

His questions stirred something deep within me. As I sat there, surrounded by the ancient trees of Kamyakavana, with this mysterious sage named Krishna beside me, I felt as though I stood on the threshold of something profound. The forest seemed to hold its breath, waiting for my answer.

"I wish to learn about the divine sight of Krishna. Apparently, he imparted this onto Arjuna." The old man's eyes narrowed as he listened to my rambling explanation about Krishna, Arjuna, and the divine sight. His weathered face contained an expression of both amusement and mild irritation.

"Young man," he began, his voice carrying a hint of exasperation, "you speak of things you clearly don't understand. The divine sight, or Vishwaroop, as you call it, is not some parlour trick that Krishna 'imparted' to Arjuna like a magician revealing his secrets."

I felt my face flush with embarrassment, but the old man continued, his voice softening slightly. "The Vishwaroop is a profound spiritual experience, a glimpse into the true nature of reality. It's not about seeing things others can't see in the physical sense. It's about perceiving the inter-connectedness of all things, the divine presence that permeates every aspect of existence."

He paused, stroking his beard thoughtfully. "In the Bhagavad Gita, Krishna reveals his universal form to Arjuna not to give him a superpower, but to help him understand the cosmic scale of existence and his role within it."

I listened intently, trying to absorb this new perspective. The old man's words were challenging my preconceptions, forcing me to think more deeply about the concepts I thought I understood.

"But," I ventured hesitantly, "why Arjuna? What made him special?"

The old man's eyes twinkled. "Ah, now you're asking the right questions.

Arjuna was chosen not because he was inherently superior, but because he had the right combination of qualities - courage, humility, wisdom, and most importantly, a deep devotion to Krishna. He was ready to receive this profound truth."

As I pondered this, a connection began to form in my mind. "Krishnaji," I said, excitement creeping into my voice, "this reminds me of something my guru was working on. He has been studying the Drake Equation in astrophysics, trying to estimate the number of civilizations in our galaxy. He believed there was a connection between this modern scientific pursuit and the ancient wisdom found in texts like the Bhagavad Gita."

The old man raised an eyebrow, intrigued. "Go on," he encouraged.

"Well, Prof. had solved six of the seven variables in the equation. He thought the final variable, which I assume may be about the longevity of civilizations, was somehow linked to spiritual advancement. He believed that truly advanced civilizations would have achieved something similar to the Vishwaroop – an understanding of their place in the cosmos."

The old man nodded slowly, a glimmer of approval in his eyes. "Your guru was a wise man. He understood that true advancement isn't just about technology, but about consciousness. The Vishwaroop isn't just about seeing the universe - it's about understanding our place within it, our connection to all things." He leaned forward, his voice dropping to a near whisper. "You see, young Siddhant, the science u talk of and the concept of Vishwaroop are both attempts to understand our place in the vast cosmos. One uses the language of mathematics and probability, the other the language of spirituality and mysticism. But at their core, they're asking the same questions: Are we alone? What is our purpose? How do we fit into the grand scheme of things?"

I felt a shiver run down my spine. Could this be the missing piece that Prof. Fitzgerald had been searching for. The link between ancient wisdom and modern science that had eluded him.

The old man continued, "Your mentor was onto something profound. The longevity of a civilization might indeed depend on its ability to achieve a collective consciousness, a shared understanding of its place in the cosmos. This is what the Vishwaroop represents on an individual level - imagine it scaled up to an entire society."

My mind was racing with possibilities. "So, you're saying that the key to solving the Drake Equation might lie in understanding the spiritual concepts described in ancient texts like the Bhagavad Gita?"

The old man smiled, a knowing look in his eyes. "I'm saying that the answers you seek might not be found solely in mathematics or in ancient texts, but in the synthesis of both. Your guru understood this. Now it's up to you to continue his work." The old man's words had given me a new perspective on my quest. The Vishwaroop wasn't just a story from an ancient text - it was a concept that could potentially hold the key to understanding our place in the universe, both scientifically and spiritually. The forest canopy rustled gently overhead as I sat cross-legged on the mossy ground, listening intently to the old man's words.

"Listen here, Siddhant," he began, his voice carrying the weight of centuries,

"Krishna wasn't just observing the universe. He was experiencing it in a way that transcended ordinary perception."

I leaned forward, captivated. The parallels between the story and my own journey were impossible to ignore. As the old man spoke, I could almost see Krishna standing beneath a star-studded sky, his gaze fixed on the heavens with a look of wonder that mirrored my own fascination with Prof. Jawahar Fitzgerald's work.

"Imagine," the old man continued, gesturing expansively, "a golden star streaking across the night sky, moving at the speed of light. Krishna not only saw it but understood its exact trajectory, the very galaxy it belonged to. This wasn't mere observation, my boy. It was a profound connection to the cosmic dance itself."

I closed my eyes for a moment, trying to picture the scene. In my mind's eye, I saw Krishna, not as some distant mythological figure, but as a flesh-and-blood being, his head tilted back, eyes wide with awe as he tracked the golden star's path across the heavens.

"It was said that Vishnu himself guided that star, a sign of recognition for Krishna's pure heart. Can you imagine it, Siddhant? The god of the universe acknowledging a mortal in such a profound way?"

I opened my eyes, finding the old man's gaze fixed intently on me. "It's like... it's like Prof. and I," I murmured, the realization dawning slowly. "He saw something in me, just as Vishnu saw something in Krishna."

The old man nodded, a knowing smile crinkling the corners of his eyes. "Precisely. And just as Krishna found Arjuna, you found your way here, to this very spot, at this very moment." As he spoke, a shaft of sunlight broke through the canopy, illuminating a small clearing nearby. Dust motes danced in the golden beam, and for a fleeting second, I could have sworn they formed the shape of a chariot.

"But how does it end?" I asked eagerly, my voice betraying my impatience.

"What happens to Krishna and Arjuna?"

The old man chuckled, shaking his head. "Ah, young one. You're jumping ahead. The story, like your own journey, has a long way to go yet."

I felt a mixture of frustration and excitement bubbling up inside me. The parallels between the ancient and my own life were undeniable, but what did it all mean? Was I truly meant to be here, in this ancient forest, talking to this enigmatic old man?

As if reading my thoughts, the old man leaned forward, his voice dropping to a near-whisper. "Listen closely, Siddhant. The Bhagavad Gita isn't just a story. It's a guide, a roadmap for the soul. Krishna and Arjuna's journey is your journey."

He paused, letting his words sink in. The forest seemed to hold its breath, the usual chorus of birds and insects falling silent. "Like Arjuna," he continued, "you stand at a crossroads. You've come far, but the greatest challenges lie ahead. The question is, are you ready to face them?"

I swallowed hard, feeling the weight of his words. The breeze picked up again, rustling the leaves overhead.

In that moment, I felt as if the entire forest was alive, watching, waiting for my response. "I... I think I am," I said, my voice stronger than I expected. "I've come this far. I owe it to Prof. Fitzgerald, to myself, to see this through."

The old man nodded approvingly. "Good. But remember, Siddhant, this journey isn't just about fulfilling a promise or solving an equation. It's about understanding your place in the cosmos, just as Arjuna had to understand his duty on the battlefield."

As he spoke, I felt a shift within myself. The doubts and uncertainties that had plagued me since arriving in Kamyakavana began to fade. In their place, a sense of purpose began to grow, as steady and strong as the ancient trees surrounding us. The old man's eyes met mine, and in them, I saw a reflection of the wisdom and determination that must have shone in Krishna's eyes as he guided Arjuna. "Your journey, like theirs, is just beginning," he said softly.

"Are you ready to see the world through new eyes, Siddhant? To understand the universe not just with your mind, but with your very soul?"

As I opened my mouth to respond, a sudden gust of wind swept through the clearing, sending leaves swirling around us in a dizzying dance. For a moment, I lost sight of the old man in the whirlwind of green and gold. When the air cleared, I found myself at the feet of the old man in the clearing, his last words echoing in my mind. I stood up slowly, brushing off my clothes. The forest around me seemed different somehow, more alive, more vibrant. At the back of my mind, I wondered who this strange person was, how was he able to guide me. But my conscious mind was going with the flow. Probably these were questions to ponder at a later time…

"You know what Siddhant…walk with me" he said, his voice gentle but firm – almost sensing my confusion. "We have a journey to make."

I followed, my mind still buzzing with questions. Why did Krishna see me as special? Why did I feel both overwhelmed and exhilarated by the weight of this cosmic responsibility? As we walked in silence, I couldn't shake the feeling that my guru was treating me like Krishna treated Arjuna. It both thrilled and terrified me - how could I, Siddhant, possibly be on the same level as these legendary figures? We walked for what seemed like hours, the forest growing denser around us. Confusion mingled with anticipation in my chest.

Finally, Krishna halted, and I stumbled to a stop beside him. "Tell me," he said, gesturing ahead, "what do you see?"

I squinted into the twilight. "Trees," I replied hesitantly. "And... a crow, I think, on that branch over there."

Krishna nodded, encouragingly. "Look closer."

I strained my eyes, searching for something, anything that might be significant.

The canopy above, the twigs scattered on the forest floor, the rough bark of the trees surrounding us. Nothing seemed out of the ordinary. Then, just as I was about to give up, I saw it. There, camouflaged against the brown stem of an enormous banyan tree, were inscriptions. Ancient writing, etched into the living wood. So faint that I missed it at first.

Excitement surged through me as I ran towards the tree. The trunk seemed to stretch endlessly upward, its branches creating a vast canopy overhead. The inscriptions spiralled up the trunk, disappearing into the foliage above. But only strong concentration made it visible. *This then was what Fitzgerald meant when he left the note "Eye of the Bird" for me!! He wanted me to concentrate on this to fathom the universe.* But as I looked at it, I realized that the language was unknown to me.

"What is this, Krishna?" I asked, tracing my fingers over the unfamiliar characters. "Is it Sanskrit?"

Krishna approached slowly, his expression unreadable. "Yes. Do you not understand Sanskrit, Siddhant?"

I felt a flush of embarrassment. "No," I admitted. "I never learned."

"Then you will have to figure it out yourself," Krishna replied, his voice carrying a hint of challenge.

Panic fluttered in my chest. "But how can I possibly learn Sanskrit in the short time I have here in Kamyakavana?" Krishna merely crossed his arms and began to walk away, leaving me alone with the inscribed tree.

"Wait!" I called after him. "Don't leave me here!"

But Krishna continued walking, his form fading into the deepening shadows of the forest. I was alone. For what felt like hours, I stared at the inscriptions, willing them to make sense. The curved lines, the intricate symbols - they were beautiful, but utterly incomprehensible to me. Yet I knew, somehow, that understanding them was crucial to unlocking the secrets of the Drake Equation. As night fell, I settled at the base of the tree, determined to decipher at least one word before sunrise. I traced the symbols with my fingers, trying to discern patterns, repeating the shapes over and over until my hand ached. I photographed the writings and tried to look it up on the internet. Slowly, maddeningly slowly, I began to make progress. A curved line that looked like an 'o' seemed to represent the sound "oo". A symbol that resembled an 'x' with a longer slash appeared frequently. I counted the words spiralling up the trunk - 112 in total.

The enormity of the task before me was overwhelming, but Krishna's words echoed in my mind: "The key to the Drake Equation is spirituality."

As dawn broke, casting a golden light through the leaves, I had deciphered the first word. My heart raced as I sounded it out: "Brahman."

Excitement surged through me. Brahman – the ultimate reality in Hinduism, the universal principle, the source of all existence.

What did this have to do with the Drake Equation? How could this ancient spiritual concept relate to the mathematical probability of extraterrestrial life? I scrambled to my feet, energized despite my sleepless night. The second word took shape under my fingers: "Consciousness." My mind raced. Consciousness and Brahman - were these the missing variables Prof. Fitzgerald had been searching for? Was the key to understanding life in the universe not just in the stars, but in the very fabric of consciousness itself? As I worked feverishly to decipher more words, the forest around me seemed to come alive. Birds called to each other in the canopy, small creatures rustled in the underbrush. For a moment, I felt as if I could sense the consciousness in every living thing around me, all connected, all part of a greater whole.

The next words emerged: "Quantum," "Entanglement," "Observer." Physics concepts intertwined with spiritual philosophies. My head spun with the implications. Hours passed, or perhaps days - time seemed to lose all meaning as I immersed myself in the ancient text. Each decoded word opened new avenues of thought, new connections between the spiritual and the scientific.

When Krishna finally returned, I was surrounded by pages of notes, my hands stained with ink, my eyes red from lack of sleep. But my mind was alight with understanding. "I think I see it now," I said, my voice hoarse from disuse. "The Drake Equation isn't just about numbers and probabilities. It's about the fundamental nature of reality itself. Consciousness, quantum entanglement, the observer effect - they're all interconnected, all part of the equation."

Krishna smiled, a look of pride in his eyes. "And now, Siddhant, you are ready to take the next step. To see not just with your eyes, but with your mind and your spirit." He led me deeper into the forest, to a clearing I hadn't seen before. In the centre stood a massive stone structure, its surface covered in intricate carvings and glowing faintly in the dim light.

"This," Krishna said, gesturing to the structure, "is the Akashic Mirror. It reflects not just light, but consciousness itself. Your task is to use it to perceive one missing variable in the Drake Equation."

I approached the mirror cautiously, my reflection distorting and shifting as I drew near.

"How does it work?" I asked, my voice barely above a whisper.

Krishna's voice was solemn. "The Akashic Mirror responds to the observer's consciousness. It will show you glimpses of the universe's fundamental truths but interpreting them... that's up to you." He placed a hand on my shoulder. "You must maintain perfect concentration for 108 minutes - no more, no less. During this time, you'll experience visions of cosmic phenomena, mathematical concepts, and spiritual truths. Your challenge is to synthesize these into a coherent understanding of the Drake Equation's missing variables."

I swallowed hard, the magnitude of the task settling over me like a heavy cloak.

"What happens if I lose concentration?" Krishna's expression grew serious.

"The mirror's power can overwhelm an unprepared mind. You might become lost in the visions, unable to distinguish reality from illusion. Some have never returned from such a state."

My heart raced, but I steeled myself. This was what I had come for, what Prof. had prepared me for. "I'm ready," I said, more confidently than I felt.

Krishna nodded. "Remember, Siddhant - what you see in the mirror is real, but also is a reflection of your own consciousness. Trust your intuition but question your assumptions. The truth lies somewhere in between."

With that, he stepped back, leaving me alone before the Akashic Mirror. I took a deep breath, focused my mind, and gazed into its shifting surface. Immediately, I was plunged into a whirlwind of images and sensations. Stars exploded into life and died in the span of heartbeats. Galaxies collided and merged. Mathematical equations danced and transformed, revealing hidden patterns. I saw the birth of consciousness in primordial oceans, watched it evolve and spread across countless worlds. Quantum fields flickered in and out of existence, their fluctuations somehow tied to the ebb and flow of thought itself. Time seemed to lose all meaning as I struggled to make sense of the cosmic tapestry unfolding before me.

Each revelation led to new questions; each answer spawned a dozen more mysteries. As the 108 minutes neared their end, I felt my concentration beginning to slip. The visions threatened to overwhelm me, to drag me into their swirling depths. With a supreme effort of will, I clung to my sense of self, to the purpose that had brought me here. In that final moment, as reality and illusion blurred, I glimpsed something profound - a unifying principle that linked consciousness, quantum mechanics, and the fundamental forces of the universe. The missing variable of the Drake Equation suddenly seemed tantalizingly close, just beyond the reach of my understanding. Then, abruptly, it was over. I found myself on my knees before the now-dormant mirror, gasping for breath, my mind reeling from the experience.

Krishna stood nearby, watching me intently. "What did you see, Siddhant?" he asked softly. As I struggled to put my experiences into words, I realized that this challenge was far from over. Deciphering the Sanskrit had been difficult, but interpreting the visions of the Akashic Mirror - and applying them to the Drake Equation - would be the true test of everything I had learned. I took a deep breath, my mind still reeling from the visions in the Akashic Mirror.

"Krishna," I began slowly, "I saw... I saw life. Not just as we know it, but life in all its possible forms.

And I saw consciousness, intertwined with the very fabric of the universe."

Krishna nodded encouragingly, his eyes sparkling with interest. "The Drake Equation," I continued, my words gaining momentum as the ideas crystallized, "it's always focused on $fl$ - the fraction of planets that develop life. But what I saw in the mirror... it changes everything." I stood up, pacing as the revelation took shape.

"We've been looking at it all wrong. Life isn't just a chemical accident waiting to happen under the right conditions. It's an inherent property of the universe itself!"

Krishna's eyebrows raised slightly, a subtle sign for me to elaborate. "The consciousness I saw... it wasn't just emerging from complex systems. It was there from the beginning, woven into the quantum fabric of reality. And life - life is the universe's way of increasing conscious complexity."

I turned to face Krishna, my eyes wide with excitement. "*Fl* isn't just about planets with the right chemical soup. It's about the universe's tendency towards consciousness expressing itself through matter. Every planet, every star, every speck of cosmic dust has the potential for life because consciousness is fundamental!"

Krishna's face broke into a wide smile.

"Go on, Siddhant. You're touching the heart of it now." Encouraged, I pressed on.

"The Drake Equation needs to be reformulated. *Fl* isn't a fraction - it's a function of time and complexity. Given enough time, the probability of life emerging approaches certainty because consciousness is always pushing towards expression." I grabbed a stick, starting to scratch equations in the dirt. "We need to incorporate quantum entanglement, the observer effect... consciousness itself as a factor in the equation. *Fl* becomes a quantum wave function, collapsing into actuality as conscious observation increases in complexity across the universe."

Krishna nodded, his eyes shining. "And what does this mean for the search for extraterrestrial life, Siddhant?"

I paused, the full implications hitting me. "It means... it means life is everywhere. Not just on Earth-like planets, but in the hearts of stars, in the void between galaxies, maybe even in dark matter itself. We've been looking for life like us, but life, driven by consciousness, could take forms we can barely imagine."

The 107- year-old sage and the awestruck student stood in the heart of the Kamyakavana.

"You've grasped an important truth, Siddhant. But remember, your professor was searching for something more concrete. The Drake Equation requires a specific value for $f_l$."

His words snapped me back to reality. Of course - we needed a number, not just a philosophical concept.

"You're right," I admitted. "But how can we quantify something so... cosmic?"

Krishna's eyes twinkled. "Think back to what you saw in the Akashic Mirror. Was there nothing there that might give us a clue?" I closed my eyes, trying to recall the swirling visions. Yes, a pattern emerged in my mind - a recurring sequence I had not focused on earlier.

"Wait," I said, my eyes snapping open. "There was a number. It kept appearing, woven into the fabric of every living system I saw."

Krishna leaned forward, intrigued. "Go on!"

I dropped to my knees, frantically scratching equations into the soft forest floor with a fallen twig. "It was a ratio," I explained, my words tumbling out as fast as my hand could move, "always the same regardless of the scale or form of life. The proportion of conscious complexity to total energy in the system." Krishna crouched beside me, his eyes following the crude symbols I was etching into the earth. Leaves and twigs scattered as I cleared more space, expanding my impromptu calculations. "If we define life as a system that increases conscious complexity over time," I continued, barely pausing for breath, "then this ratio... it's the key to calculating $f\ell$!"

My hands were soon covered in dirt, but I hardly noticed.

The forest floor became my chalkboard, the twig my pen. Equations sprawled across the ground, connecting like the roots of the ancient trees surrounding us.

Krishna watched in silence, occasionally nodding as if confirming my train of thought. The sounds of the forest - birdsong, rustling leaves, distant water – faded into the background as I lost myself in the calculations. Time seemed to lose all meaning. The sun shifted overhead, dappling the ground with ever-changing patterns of light and shadow. I worked tirelessly, cross-referencing the crude markings with everything I knew about life on Earth and the principles of quantum mechanics. Finally, I sat back on my heels, my hands trembling slightly as I surveyed the sprawling mathematical landscape I'd created on the forest floor. I looked up at Krishna, my voice hoarse.

"Krishna, if this is correct... $f\ell$ isn't just probability. It's a universal constant."

He knelt down, examining the equations etched into the earth with intense focus.

"And the value?" he asked softly.

I swallowed hard, my throat dry. "0.577214," I said. "To six decimal places, at least. It's approximately equal to the inverse of Euler's number $e$."

Krishna's eyes widened slightly - the most surprise I'd ever seen him show.

"Remarkable," he murmured. "Do you understand what this means, Siddhant?"

As the implications sank in, I felt a surge of excitement tinged with awe. Here, in an ancient forest, using nothing but a stick and the ground beneath my feet, and a saviour in Krishna, I had possibly unlocked one of the universe's fundamental secrets.

The forest seemed to hold its breath as Krishna's revelation sank in. I stood there, rooted to the spot, my mind reeling from the implications of what I'd just said.

The air was thick with the scent of damp earth and ancient wood, a natural incense that seemed to intensify the gravity of the moment.

"My professor....knew you? All this time?" I managed to stammer, my voice barely above a whisper.

Krishna's eyes twinkled, a mixture of mischief and ancient wisdom. "Indeed, Siddhant. Your guru and I shared a long history."

Before I could bombard him with the thousand questions bubbling up inside me, Krishna held up a hand, silencing me with a gentle but firm gesture. "Remember, I told you I hadn't spoken for three months? That's because the last person I spoke to was Jawahar himself."

My jaw dropped.

The pieces were falling into place, forming a picture I could scarcely believe.

"But... how? Why?" My voice was a blend of disbelief and curiosity, each question adding weight to the mystery. Instead of answering directly, Krishna beckoned me to follow. We walked deeper into the forest, the thick canopy above us filtering the sunlight into a green, ethereal glow. The light danced on the forest floor, creating patterns that seemed to move with a life of their own. The air was cool and filled with the sounds of unseen birds and the rustling of leaves, a symphony of nature that contrasted sharply with the whirlwind of thoughts in my head.

After a few minutes, we came to a clearing. Krishna pointed to a nearby tree, its trunk scarred with dozens of small marks. "Look closely," he instructed, his voice carrying a hint of anticipation.

I approached the tree, running my fingers over the marks. They were evenly spaced, about a centimetre apart. The texture of the bark under my fingers felt rough and ancient.

"Are these... arrow marks?" I asked, turning to Krishna.

He nodded, a small smile playing on his lips. "Your guru was quite the archer."

No!! this was something he never revealed to me.

He led me to another tree, this one bearing similar marks, but closer together. The precision and consistency of the marks spoke of years of practice and a level of skill that seemed almost supernatural. And finally, we came to an enormous banyan tree, its trunk pierced by a single, perfect hole right through its centre.

"Seven years," Krishna said softly. "That's how long he practiced here." I stared at the hole, trying to imagine my former high school physics teacher, the frail old man I knew, drawing a bow with enough strength and precision to shoot an arrow clean through a tree trunk. It seemed impossible, a feat beyond human capability.

"But why?" I asked, turning back to Krishna. "What did archery have to do with his work on the Drake Equation?"

My mind was struggling to connect the dots between these seemingly disparate elements of the Prof.'s life. Krishna settled himself on a large root, patting the space beside him. I sat down, feeling the rough bark beneath my hands, grounding me as my mind swam with questions. The forest around us seemed to close in, creating an intimate cocoon for the conversation.

"Jawahar was fascinated by the forest and the creatures in the forest," Krishna began, his voice taking on a rhythmic, almost hypnotic quality. "He would spend hours observing the birds here in the forest. The eagle soaring high above, its keen eyes scanning the ground. The mother bird in her nest, waiting for her chicks to take their first flight."

I could almost see it - notebook in his hand, peering up at the forest canopy with the same intensity he brought to his equations. His figure, now more vivid in my mind, blended with the serene surroundings of the forest, creating an image of a man deeply connected to the world around him.

"He was particularly fascinated by the bird's eye," Krishna continued. "The way it sees everything from above. The birds view is holistic - In a way, he saw it as... godlike."

A cool breeze rustled through the leaves, sending a shiver down my spine. The imagery of the bird's eye, all-seeing and omniscient, resonated deeply within me.

"So, he was trying to... what? Develop a bird's-eye view of the universe?" Krishna's smile deepened, his eyes twinkling with a knowing light. "Who knows? But year after year, I would see him here, bow in hand, arrow aimed at that banyan tree. We would lock eyes, share a slight smile, and then he would release the arrow."

I tried to picture it - my brilliant, eccentric mentor, standing in this very clearing, trying to pierce the heart of a tree as if it held the secrets of the cosmos. The scene felt both surreal and profoundly real, an intersection of the tangible and the mystical.

"But you said you spoke to him three months ago," I pressed. "After seven years of silence."

Krishna's expression grew solemn. "Yes. He came to me as I sat by the river. He told me a boy would visit soon - maybe in a week, maybe in years. 'wheatish skin, thick black hair, big eyes that seem to observe all,' he said." I unconsciously reached up to touch my eyes, wondering if they really did observe that much. The description, though humorous, added a touch of human warmth to Prof. Fitzgerald's memory.

"How is that possible?" I whispered. "How could he have known I would come?"

Krishna's gaze seemed to pierce right through me.

"Because he saw something in you that he recognized in himself. Insatiable curiosity, a drive to understand the unknown."

A lump formed in my throat. "I...I didn't even know he had been here in the forest until I arrived here." The realization that he was no longer here to share the moment brought a lump in my throat.

Krishna nodded sadly. "His health had been failing for years. He knew the end was near."

"Did he tell you anything about his work?" I asked, leaning forward eagerly.

"About the Drake Equation?"

Krishna's expression grew serious. "Siddhant, what you're asking about - it was his life's work. Twenty-seven years he dedicated to that equation. It consumed him, drove him to the brink of madness at times."

The weight of responsibility settled on my shoulders like a physical thing. I realized then the true magnitude of what Prof. Fitzgerald had entrusted me with. This wasn't just about finishing an equation or solving a puzzle. It was about carrying forward a legacy, about fulfilling the dream of a man who had dedicated his entire life to understanding the cosmos.

"You need to prove yourself worthy of your own work, not just Jawahar Fitzgerald's. How can I simply hand you his life's efforts when you can forge your own path?"

I opened my mouth to protest, to explain how much Prof. Fitzgerald's work meant to me, but Krishna held up a hand, silencing me with a gentle but firm gesture.

"You found *FI*, didn't you?

"But not by myself. All this time, it's been you and Prof. guiding me. Not to forget a beautiful girl. Now I struggle to stand on my own feet." My words stung, piercing through defences, but I knew there was truth in them. I looked down at my hands, calloused from my time in the forest, yet still so young and untested compared to Krishna's weathered palms. The contrast was stark, a reminder of how much I still had to learn and grow.

"You are young," Krishna's voice gentle but firm. "You are not even a man yet. If you are so harsh on yourself, can you ever be happy?" He paused, then asked, "Tell me, young Sid, when you look in the mirror every morning, what do you see?"

I thought hard, searching for an answer, but my mind went blank. "I... I don't know," I admitted, realizing with a start how little I truly knew myself. The admission felt like peeling away a layer of my being, exposing vulnerabilities I hadn't acknowledged before.

Krishna's eyes softened, filled with an understanding that transcended words. "It's okay. I see you trying really hard. When you are your guru's age, you will be able to answer that question."

Frustration bubbled up inside me. "Krishna, what do I have to do to be worthy of receiving his work?" I asked, my voice tinged with desperation. I wanted so badly to prove myself, to feel worthy of the legacy Fitzgerald had left behind.

"Your own," he replied simply. "This is your journey. Why are you stuck on completing his? Prof. Fitzgerald is gone, but your life is just beginning. When the time is right, you will uncover what you want to. For now, go with the flow."

I felt tears pricking at the corners of my eyes. The raw emotion of the moment was almost too much to bear. "But... I don't believe I can do it on my own. I need help. I need his work."

Krishna shook his head slowly, his expression one of both compassion and firmness. "I understand you want me to help you, but guess what? I couldn't, even if I wanted to."

"What does that mean?" I asked, confusion replacing my frustration. The idea that Krishna, with all his wisdom, couldn't help me was both unsettling and liberating.

"I don't know where those values of the equation are," Krishna admitted. "But I hope your desperation has led you to something fulfilling now. Go, get out of this forest and write your own story."

As his words sank in, I felt a shift within myself. The forest around us seemed to breathe with me, the ancient trees witness to this moment of transformation. The realization that the answers I sought were not out there, but within me, was both daunting and empowering.

"Life can be a rollercoaster at times," Krishna said softly, "but every episode teaches a lesson. You were chasing shadows, Siddhant. This entire trip... it was meant to be a tiny awakening, to turn your life 180 degrees."

I looked up at him, seeing not just the wise old man, but a mirror reflecting my own potential. "You made me realize," I said slowly, "that attaining moksha comes in different ways. For you, leaving your past life and starting anew in Kamyakavana was part of it." Krishna nodded, a smile playing at the corners of his lips. The serene acceptance in his eyes was a testament to the peace he had found in his own journey.

"And for me," I continued, the realization dawning, "if I ask myself what moksha is... creating my own road to completing the Drake Equation would be it."

The forest seemed to hum with approval. Birds called overhead, their songs a melodious backdrop to this moment of clarity. A warm breeze rustled through the leaves, carrying with it the scents of earth and life.

I stood up, feeling taller somehow, more grounded in my own sense of self. "Thank you, Krishna," I said, my voice steady and clear. "I think... I think I'm ready to leave now."

Krishna's eyes twinkled with pride and something else... perhaps a hint of the divine spark that had guided Prof. Fitzgerald all those years ago.

"Remember Siddhant, the journey is yours. The equation is just a part of it. Go forth and discover not just the secrets of the universe, but the depths of your own soul."

As I turned to leave the clearing, I felt a profound sense of both ending and beginning. The quest was transforming into something uniquely my own. The Drake Equation still beckoned, but now it was a challenge I chose to accept, not a burden I was obligated to bear. With each step away from Krishna and deeper into my own future, I felt the whispers of the forest fading, replaced by the quiet certainty of my own resolve. The path ahead was long and uncertain, but for the first time since I'd arrived in Kamyakavana, I was truly ready to walk it. The forest seemed to embrace me one last time as I made my way back through the dense foliage. Each step felt like a farewell to a chapter of my life, while simultaneously welcoming a new, uncharted journey. The sunlight filtering through the leaves cast a golden glow on the path ahead, symbolizing hope and the promise of discovery.

As I walked, I couldn't help but reflect on the experiences that had brought me here. The long hours spent in contemplation, the nights under the stars, and the silent companionship of nature had all contributed to this moment of awakening.

The forest, with its ancient wisdom, had been both a sanctuary and a teacher.

I thought about Prof. Fitzgerald the brilliant, eccentric mentor who had guided me through the complexities of the Drake Equation. His passion for understanding the universe had been infectious, but it was his unwavering belief in my potential that had truly inspired me. Now, standing at the threshold of my own journey, I felt a deep sense of gratitude for the lessons he had imparted. Krishna's words echoed in my mind, a reminder that the journey was mine to shape. The Drake Equation was no longer just an abstract mathematical problem; it was a symbol of the quest for knowledge and self-discovery. It represented the intersection of science and philosophy, a bridge between the known and the unknown. I realized that the answers I sought were not just about solving an equation, but about understanding the larger mysteries of existence.

The journey ahead would require patience, perseverance, and an open mind. There would be challenges and setbacks, but each step would bring me closer to a deeper understanding of both the universe and me.

As I reached the edge of the forest, the world beyond seemed both familiar and new. The sounds of everyday life mingled with the lingering echoes of the forest, creating a symphony of past and present. I took a deep breath, feeling the weight of expectation lift, replaced by a sense of anticipation and excitement. The forest had been my crucible, a place of transformation where I had shed the weight of expectations and emerged with a renewed sense of purpose. As I ventured into the unknown, I carried with me the wisdom of Krishna, the legacy of Prof. Fitzgerald, and the unshakable belief in my own potential. The journey ahead was long, but I was ready. The universe was waiting to reveal its secrets, and I was prepared to uncover them, one step at a time.

As I reached the edge of the forest I recollected the last words of Krishna… as he had placed a hand on my shoulder, his touch warm and reassuring. "Jawahar believed in you, Siddhant. He saw in you the potential to complete what he started. But remember, the journey ahead is long. You have three more variables to uncover before you can tackle the final one."

"Where do I start?" I had asked.

"With the first step, of course. And then the next. And the next after that. The universe will reveal its secrets in due time, Siddhant. Don't be ruthless to yourself. Your only task for now is to be ready when it does."

# Chapter 8

# PARALLEL LIVES, DIVERGENT PATHS

I spent the rest of my formative years in the United States, a land that moulded my character and expanded my horizons. Majoring in astrophysics at Berkeley University was a dream I never thought I deserved, but one I relentlessly pursued.

The vast campus, with its towering redwoods and bustling student life, became my new world. Einstein's quotes adorned the walls of my classrooms, and each day felt like an adventure, filled with the excitement of learning something new. However, my journey to this point wasn't without its struggles. My IIT dreams never materialized, despite being ranked in the JEE. Perhaps fate had other plans for me, something better knocking at my door. Berkeley, with its blend of tradition and innovation, was my second chance. As I walked down the famous pathways of the university, I felt a thrill knowing I was part of a legacy of great minds. Berkeley was more than just a place of learning; it was a vibrant community that pushed me to grow in ways I never anticipated. The campus buzzed with intellectual energy.

The Sather Tower, or Campanile, stood as a beacon, its bells echoing through the campus, marking the passage of time. Sproul Plaza was always alive with activity—students debating, musicians playing, and activists rallying for various causes. It was here that I learned the power of voice and the importance of standing up for one's beliefs.

One of the most memorable experiences was the annual Big Game against Stanford. The entire campus buzzed with anticipation. Students painted their faces blue and gold, the school colours, and marched together to the stadium, chanting fight songs. The rivalry was intense, but it was all in good spirit.

I remember the surge of adrenaline as our team scored the winning touchdown, the crowd erupting in cheers. In that moment, I felt a deep sense of belonging and pride. Berkeley was also a melting pot of cultures and ideas. The International House was a hub for students from around the world, where we shared our traditions and learned from each other. I made friends from every corner of the globe, each bringing a piece of their homeland with them. We celebrated Diwali, Chinese New Year, and countless other festivals together, each one a vibrant display of unity in diversity. The university's location in the Bay Area provided endless opportunities for exploration. Weekends were often spent hiking in the nearby hills, with breathtaking views of the Golden Gate Bridge and the Pacific Ocean. San Francisco, just a short ride away, was a city of endless wonders—its steep streets, historic cable cars, and eclectic neighbourhoods offering a stark contrast to the tranquil beauty of Berkeley.

My classes were challenging, often pushing me to my limits. In the physics labs, I spent countless nights working on experiments, the cold, sterile smell of the lab becoming almost comforting. The equations on the whiteboards seemed endless, yet each one was a step closer to understanding the mysteries of the universe. My professors were both intimidating and inspiring, their passion for the subject infectious. They didn't just teach—they challenged, provoked, and inspired us to think critically and creatively.

One professor, Dr. Hamilton, stood out. His lectures were legendary, often leaving us in awe. He had a way of making complex theories accessible, using everyday analogies that made the most abstract concepts click. I remember one particularly tough day; he pulled me aside after class.

"You seem troubled," he said, his eyes piercing but kind.

"It's just...sometimes it feels like too much," I admitted.

He smiled. "That's the point. The beauty of science is in its complexity. Embrace the struggle. It's what makes the breakthroughs so rewarding."

Outside the classroom, Berkeley offered a world of opportunities. The sports culture was strong, with varied events that brought the whole campus together. I often found myself in the bleachers, cheering for our teams, feeling a part of something bigger. The camaraderie was infectious, a welcome break from the rigors of my studies.

My final year at Berkeley was intense. The pressures of graduate school had made me almost forget my past, the painful memories, and the lingering guilt over events I couldn't control. Nightmares of being responsible for my mentor's death with the pressures I had brought upon him, and then let him down haunted me, but by the age of 24, I had matured. Life had a way of pushing me forward, despite the shadows of the past.

One day, as I strolled by the famous trial field of the campus, a vibrant poster caught my eye.

"Prove you're the best marksman!" it proclaimed, with an image of an A360 pistol, just like the one I used during my shooting days. Nostalgia washed over me, memories of competitions, and camaraderie with friends like Ronald and Avantika. They were always there, supporting me, and in those moments, I felt a surge of confidence.

Three days later, I found myself at the competition, surrounded by seasoned marksmen and curious onlookers. There was another section put up for onlookers who wished to try their hand. A senior of mine, Joe, whom I had interacted with a couple of times, and who had a heavy southern accent was encouraging people to try their hand. Soon he approached me.

"Hey there, you a good shot?" he asked, his voice rough but friendly. I was taken aback, unsure what to say.

"A good what?" I replied, nervous sweat forming on my brow.

"A good shot. Can you shoot?" he clarified, his tattooed arms crossing over his chest.

"Yes," I answered, trying to hide my anxiety.

He handed me a pistol, and I instinctively lined up a target. "Hold on there, Sid. You need eye protection," he said, handing me a pair of safety glasses. I put them on, feeling a rush of familiarity as I gripped the gun. The target seemed less than 10 meters away, a distance that once felt so easy. With my left hand resting in my pocket, I raised my right arm, the pistol steady. I took a deep breath, closed my eyes, and pulled the trigger. The smell of gunpowder filled the air, and I was transported back to my teen years, the days of rigorous training and exhilarating competitions. When I opened my eyes, I saw my shot had hit the centre of the target.

People around me stared in astonishment. "On your first try?" one of them exclaimed.

"Well... I guess it came naturally," I said, my confidence growing.

"It takes a special eye to hit the centre on your first shot," Joe said, impressed.

"Yes, like the eye of a bird," I repeated, smiling at the memory, but of course he didn't understand the reference.

"So, what's your incentive for hosting this shooting competition?" I asked, curious.

He shrugged. "Just organized a little something for fun. Where are you from, anyway?"

"India," I replied.

"The land of science, huh? You must be smart as hell."

I chuckled. "It's been quite a journey. The people here are friendly, and the teachers... well, they're some of the best I've ever had. But the ones back home in India, they had a way of pushing us through uncomfortable situations, really bringing out our best."

He seemed intrigued. "What kind of uncomfortable situations?"

I thought for a moment, recalling the times I felt lonely in my life, the time I lost Krishna. How was I supposed to share my innermost thoughts and feelings with a stranger? Couple of casual interactions didn't qualify him as a confidante. And yet, it was with this neutral person with whom the outpourings came. They would not judge me, so it was easy to open up. I found myself unburdening to him.

"There were times I felt incredibly lonely," I began, the memories flooding back. "I lost my friend philosopher and guide, Krishna. It felt like a part of me was gone."

"Krishna?" he asked, his curiosity doubled. "I've heard of him," he said, surprising me. "Isn't he one of those million gods you guys have?"

I nodded, smiling at his misunderstanding. "Krishna is a common name in India. But yes, there is a deity named Krishna. It's fascinating that you know that."

He laughed. "I do know a bit. Like Robert Oppenheimer, the inventor of the atomic bomb. He was quite into your culture, wasn't he? Hinduism and the Bhagavad Gita?"

I was taken aback. "Wait, what? Was he?"

He continued, "Oppenheimer often quoted the Bhagavad Gita. He said it gave him great difficulty but also great clarity when he built the atomic bomb."

I was intrigued. "But how? There's no element of man or physics in the Bhagavad Gita."

"Actually, there is," he replied. "We learned it in our final year course ME2004.

The concept of duty, the idea of karma—these are all elements that play into how we view our work and our responsibilities."

I was stunned. "You learned this in a theoretical physics class?"

"Yes. It's amazing how interconnected everything is. How do you not know about your own culture?"

"I guess I never thought it would be helpful. But now I realize it helped the father of the atomic bomb."

He looked at me intently, as if deciding whether to share something significant.

"You know, Oppenheimer quoted a verse from the Bhagavad Gita when he saw the first successful test of the atomic bomb. He said, *'In battle, in forest, at the precipice in the mountains, on the dark great sea, in the midst of javelins and arrows, in sleep, in confusion, in the depths of shame, the good deeds a man has done before, defend him.'*"

I was shocked. "Oppenheimer said that?"

He nodded. "Yes, he believed it helped him reconcile his actions and the guilt he carried. It's powerful, isn't it?" I was speechless. The verse echoed in my mind.

If Oppenheimer was talking about defending himself, surely, he must have been guilty first. I related Oppenheimer's situation to Prof. Fitzgerald's. I remembered visiting his brother, Jehangir Fitzgerald, and how he tried to hide his guilt encompassed past. There was falling apart between the brothers, I assumed because Jehangir did not want his brother to be involved in his research.

Returning to my dorm room, I searched through my contacts. I needed to reach out to Lakshmi, Prof.'s brother's wife. We had exchanged numbers when I had visited them to deliver the news of his brother's death.

Prof. Fitzgerald, had often seemed burdened, taking pills to cope with his past. I dialled Lakshmi's number, hoping she could help piece together the puzzle of Fitzgerald's guilt and perhaps shed light on my own struggles. Lakshmi answered on the third ring, her voice calm but curious.

"Hello?" Laxmi faltered; her voice as uncertain as if she were trying to recall a distant memory. "It's been so long. Why do you call now? Jehangir, he's not here. Gone to the well... to fetch more water. Always busy, that man. Why you call after all these years?" she said in her broken English.

I felt my breath catch in my throat, memories flooding back of the last time I'd seen Jahangir and Laxmi. The bamboo-laden house in Panchgani, the scent of 'chai' in the air, and the burden of the news I'd brought them about Jawahar's passing. The last time I'd been in their house, I was just a boy, full of questions and a burning curiosity about the world. Now, all these years later, I had just one question left, and I wasn't sure I was ready to hear the answer.

"I need to speak with him, Laxmi," I managed, trying to keep the urgency out of my voice. My free hand fidgeted with a pen on my desk, a nervous habit I'd never quite shaken. "Please, when he returns… could you pass him the phone? It's important. There's something I need to ask him, something that's bothering me." There was a pause on the other end, filled only by the distant sounds of life on the other side of the world—the creaking of bamboo, the faint rustle of leaves in the wind, and Laxmi's hesitant breathing. For a moment, I wondered if she had hung up, or whether my request had been too forward. But then she spoke again, her voice softer this time, almost apologetic.

"Strange coincidence, no?" Laxmi mused, her broken English somehow making her words more poignant. "Last time you came, he was also at the well. Always fetching water, always busy. Life here, it not change much. But you… you sound different now. Older, maybe sadder. But… I will tell him you called. You wait, yes?"

The line went quiet again, and I listened intently, straining to hear any sign of Jehangir's return. My mind wandered, dredging up memories I hadn't touched in years—the house in Panchgani, the heaviness of the heart – laden with the shock of Fitzgerald's death. I remembered the day I'd first met Jawahar in class, how his eyes had lit up when he had spoken of the cosmos, of the mysteries that lay hidden in the vast expanse of space. And I remembered the day I'd had to tell Jehangir that his brother was gone.

I was so lost in thought that I almost missed the sound of a deep voice on the other end of the line, familiar and yet changed, as if time itself had etched its mark upon it. "Ha bolo?"

The raspy timbre of Jahangir's voice sent a jolt through me, bringing me sharply back to the present.

"Yes, Jehangir Saab, it's me… Siddhant," I said, struggling to keep my voice steady. My heart was pounding so loudly I was sure he could hear it through the phone. I exchanged inane pleasantries and then blurted, "I have just one question. You left me hanging the last time we spoke, and I need to know… what caused the rift between you and your brother?" There was a long silence on the other end, so long that I began to wonder if the call had been disconnected.

I held my breath, listening, and then he spoke again, his voice low and measured, as if he was choosing his words carefully.

"Why now, Siddhant? Why ask me this after so many years?" The weight of unspoken history hung between us, palpable even across the miles separating us. I hesitated, my mind racing. How could I explain the burning curiosity that had plagued me for so long? The need to understand, to piece together the fragments of a story that had haunted me since being a teenage.

The question had been a constant companion, always there at the back of my mind, demanding answers.

"I… I can't explain it, Jehangir Saab," I finally said, my voice barely above a whisper. "But I need to know. It's like a puzzle with a missing piece, and I can't rest until I find it. Please, I know it might be painful, but I need to understand." He sighed heavily, and for a moment, all I could hear was his laboured breathing. Then, without warning, the line went dead. I stared at the phone in disbelief, the dial tone buzzing in my ear like an angry insect.

"Hello? Jehangir Saab?" I called out, but it was useless. He had hung up. Frustration welled up inside me. I had been so close to getting the answers I'd sought for years, only to have them snatched away at the last moment. I slammed the phone down, my hand shaking with a mix of frustration and disappointment. For the next three days, I was a bundle of nerves. I couldn't focus on my work, couldn't sleep properly. Every time the phone rang, I jumped, hoping it would be Jehangir, but it never was. I tried calling back several times, but Laxmi always answered, her voice growing increasingly annoyed as she told me Jehangir wasn't available. On the third day, just as I was beginning to lose hope, the phone rang. It was late in the evening, and I had been staring absently at a stack of graded papers on my desk. I picked up the receiver, not daring to hope.

"Hello?" I said, my voice cautious.

"Siddhant." It was Jehangir's voice, gravelly and tired, but unmistakable. "I... I apologize for hanging up on you. It was... difficult to revisit those memories. But I will tell you our story because eight years ago you took the effort to come to my place and share with me the news of my brother's demise."

Relief flooded through me, followed quickly by a renewed sense of anticipation.

"Very well, Siddhant," Jahangir said finally, his voice tinged with resignation. "I will tell you, but you must listen, and you must understand… it is not an easy story to tell. It's a tale of love and betrayal, of dreams and disappointments. Are you sure you're ready to hear it?"

I nodded, even though I knew he couldn't see me, and I settled into my chair, ready to listen. My hand reached for a notebook and pen, ready to capture every word. This was the moment I had been waiting for, the answers I had sought for so long.

"I'm ready, Jahangir Saab," I said, my voice steady now.

Jehangir began to speak, his voice mirroring years of pain, regret, and, above all, a deep and abiding love for his brother. As he talked, I could feel the story coming to life, the characters stepping out of the past and into the present.

"We grew up in a mixed household" he began, his voice steady and strong.

"English and Mother India. Two worlds, colliding within the walls of our home. My father, an Englishman with his colonial airs, and my mother, a proud Indian woman who never let go of her heritage. They were like oil and water, never truly mixing, always in conflict."

I closed my eyes, trying to picture the world Jehangir was describing. I could smell the spices from the kitchen mixing with the scent of English tea, a metaphor for the cultural clash that defined their home.

"My father was a playboy," Jehangir continued, his voice growing colder as he spoke of the man who had raised him.

"It was hard for Jawahar and me. We didn't understand it then, but we could feel the tension, the unhappiness. It was like a dark cloud hanging over our home, always there, always casting a shadow over everything. We sought refuge in each other. We spent hours sharing our secrets, our dreams. We talked about the future, about escaping the confines of our home and making something of ourselves. We dreamed of the stars, Siddhant, of unravelling the mysteries of the universe. But the world… the world is not so kind, Siddhant," Jehangir said, his voice growing hard.

"People take your kindness for granted. They see it as weakness, and they use it against you. I learned this lesson the hard way, and it cost me more than I could have ever imagined."

I could feel the tension building in him, the sense that something was about to break, that the bond between the brothers was about to be tested in a way that it had never been before. My pen hovered over the paper, ready to capture the words that would explain the rift that had torn these two brothers apart.

"And then, fourteen years later, in 1999, it happened," Jahangir said, his voice low and filled with a deep, simmering anger. "I found out that Jawahar had stolen my doctoral dissertation. The equation I had worked on for years, the one that was supposed to be my crowning achievement… he took it from me. The betrayal, Siddhant, it was like a knife to my heart."

A chill ran down my spine as Jehangir spoke. I could not imagine my professor, who transformed me, being a thief.

"How did you find out?" I asked, my voice barely above a whisper, dreading the answer but needing to know.

"We both majored in astrophysics in graduate school," Jehangir said, his words measured and deliberate. "We both had the same goal, the same dream. To achieve a doctorate, to make a name for ourselves in the world of science. But when time came to choose a topic for our research, I chose the one that had fascinated me for years." I could hear the passion in his voice as he continued describing the Drake equation.

"I first heard about it in Carl Sagan's Cosmos. *'Humanity, having progressed to the moon, still cannot quite catch this irate, Mathematical precision-based equation. One to solve the biggest mystery of humanity: Are we alone?'* Sagan had said in his book.

I too had been reading books since young. But Sagan always caught my attention too. I took a deep breath, absorbing the weight of Jehangir's words. The Drake Equation, a mathematical concept that had tantalized astrophysicists for decades, had been at the centre of this tale of brotherly love, betrayal, and redemption. As I listened to Jehangir recount his story, I couldn't help but reflect on my own journey with this enigmatic equation.

"I took on the challenge of the Drake Equation," he continued, "I was one step closer to the truth, and it felt like a small victory."

The memory of those early days of my research flooded back, the excitement of discovery, the late nights poring over data and calculations.

Jehangir went on, "After years of searching, I finally found a clue—$Fp$. That should have been a moment of triumph, but instead, everything spiralled out of control. My own blood proved to be treacherous." I realised that the bitterness of that memory still lingered in him, even after all these years.

"But ever since I was betrayed, I lost my passion and my goal."

The defeat in his voice was palpable, a stark contrast to the brilliant, ambitious scientist he must have once been. My heart ached for Jehangir.

Here was a man who had dedicated his life to his research, who had dreamed of finding out the mysteries of the universe, only to have it all stolen from him. The injustice of it all burned in my chest.

"It is unbelievable that my professor stole your topic," I ventured, trying to digest this news.

Jehangir agreed, his gaze distant, lost in memories of a time long past. "He did use my findings on $FP$ as an uplift to achieve $Fl$, $Fi$, $Fc$," he explained, his voice a mixture of pride and pain. "When I saw the news of his research papers published in the Times of India, with JJ. Fitzgerald written as the author, it felt like a knife in my chest. I should have been in that position, receiving the accolades, but instead, I was left in the shadows."

I could hear the bitterness in his voice, the pain of watching someone else reap the rewards of his hard work. But there was a piece of the puzzle that seemed odd.

"Why did he write it as JJ?" I asked, curiously.

Jehangir made a deep, weary sound, "Because in an interview with Science, he finally admitted to the world that his research wasn't his alone —it was mine too. Jehangir and Jawahar Fitzgerald."

My heart sank at those words, a wave of realization crashing over me. He may have taken his brother's ideas, but he did do the decent thing finally. He gave justice, and recognition—not just to himself, but to Jehangir too. He might have been a thief, but an honourable one eventually. However, I wondered whether the means justified the end. Was the professor right in what he had done? The complexity of their relationship, the depth of their bond, suddenly became clear to me.

"Although I appreciated his words," Jehangir continued, his voice thick with emotion. "But I couldn't bring myself to go back, to apologize, to look him in the eye and tell him to go on, and do it for us. The hatred in my heart was too much to bear." The pain in his voice was raw, a wound that had never truly healed. "And then one day, you came to me with the news of his untimely death. I held my emotions back that day, but inside, I wanted to cry. I wanted to cry my heart out, cry my soul out, because my brother, who had given everything – even his conscience - to fight for our place in the world, was gone."

Listening to Jehangir speak so intensely, my own heart ached. The tragedy of their story, the missed opportunities for reconciliation, the love that had turned to bitterness and then to regret—it was almost too much to bear.

"I didn't know this meant so much to you," I whispered, my voice choked with emotion. And then, as if a switch had been flipped, I felt a surge of determination. "I've been a fool all this time," I admitted, "thinking I would act on the equation someday. But that 'someday' is now."

My words hung in the air, a promise to myself and to Jehangir. "All this while I was chasing someone else's work, but now I promise you, Jehangir, I will finish what you started."

As I spoke, I felt a sense of clarity washing over me, as if the fog of uncertainty that had clouded my path for so long was finally lifting.

"I now understand what Krishna told me in the Kamyakavana—create your path. All this time, I only heard what he said, but now I feel it."

The wisdom of those ancient words, spoken in a forest clearing so long ago, suddenly took on a new meaning.

"I will complete the equation, for myself, for you, and for prof. Jawahar Fitzgerald."

I felt a renewed sense of purpose wash over me. It was as if all the pieces of my life—my childhood dreams, my academic pursuits, my relationship with Jawahar Sir, and now this conversation with Jehangir— were finally falling into place. As our conversation drew to a close, I felt a sense of peace settling over me. The weight of unfinished business, of unanswered questions that had burdened me for so long, began to lift. In its place was a new sense of purpose, a clear vision of the path ahead.

# Chapter 9

# DUAL DISCOVERY

I knew that to tackle something as complex as the Drake Equation, I needed to prepare myself both mentally and physically. To get my head back into the astrophysics frenzy, I decided to return to my original passion—rifle shooting. It might seem like an odd choice, but to me, the connection was clear.

"I knew that to master mathematical precision, I first had to master my mind's focus," I explained to my brother who was working in New York and who asked me why I needed to get back to rifle shooting, "and there was no better way to do that than to revisit my childhood love."

The shooting range became my sanctuary, a place where the world narrowed down to just me, my rifle, and the target. Each shot was a lesson in focus, in blocking out distractions, in achieving perfect alignment of body and mind.

Once again, I felt the passion, a drive that I hadn't felt since going one on one with Ronald. His skill with a rifle had reminded me of the precision and focus required in astrophysics, the way each variable in the equation needed to be carefully considered and balanced. I found myself diving deeper into my studies of the Drake Equation.

The two pursuits—marksmanship and astrophysics—began to intertwine in my mind, each informing and enhancing the other. The focus I gained from shooting helped me concentrate on complex calculations, while the mental agility required for the equation improved my performance on the range. Life has a way of connecting the dots for us. Sometimes, we just need to step back and see the bigger picture.

I turned back to the range, my rifle feeling both familiar and somehow new in my hands. Each shot now carried a different weight, a different meaning. It wasn't just about hitting the target anymore; it was about aligning my heart, my mind, and my purpose. As I stood at the Berkeley shooting range, the AK in my hands felt like an extension of my own body. The weapons here were far more sophisticated than those I'd used back in India, a stark reminder of the disparity in funding and resources between our countries. The AK's protruding butt and noiseless barrel created a symphony of precision engineering. As I loaded a bullet, the clicking sound was music to my ears - a familiar melody that transported me back to my youth. I positioned myself, the rifle's stock nestling perfectly into my shoulder, my elbow resting on my hip. The stance was familiar, yet different.

Back at Savarkar Academy in Mumbai, I'd always had to compensate for the weapon's imperfections, adjusting my aim constantly. But here, the gun's stock grip was incredibly tight, fitting into my palm like it was custom-made for me. It was no wonder the United States dominated Olympic shooting events - their training facilities and equipment were light years ahead of the rest of the world. Taking a deep breath, I squeezed the trigger. The lack of recoil was astounding - the gun barely moved as the bullet left the barrel. My first shot hit a nine, and I couldn't help but think back to my shootout with Ronald, where I'd botched my chances at the end.

The white circles on the target seemed to mock me, a reminder of past failures. But something was different today. As I continued to fire, the numbers on the target became a blur: 9, 10, 8, 9, 9, 9, 8, 9, 10, 9, 8, 7, 9, 6, 9. The nine circle was no longer a circle, but a ragged hole punctured by my barrage of bullets. Yet, for the first time in my life, I realized I was shooting without pressure. I had no ambition to be the best shooter in the world or to compete in the Olympics. I was shooting for the pure love of the sport, just as Professor Fitzgerald had practiced archery. As I watched the bullets fly through the scope, traveling at 800 km/hour and reaching the target in a hundredth of a second, I marvelled at the science behind it. The rifling - the helical grooves inside the barrel - imparted a spin to the bullet, transforming it into a miniature gyroscope. This spin stabilized its flight, ensuring it travelled as straight as possible.

"Gyroscope," I mumbled to myself, standing in the middle of the Berkeley shooting range. My mind wandered to Physicswallah, or Alakh Pandey as Professor Fitzgerald knew him. He had once explained how gyroscopes were the nucleus of automated steering systems in aircraft, missiles, and torpedoes. The principle behind gyroscopes fascinated me - its rigidity in space and precision.

A gyroscope tended to maintain its orientation, resisting changes to its axis of rotation.

This property, known as rigidity in space, is what made gyroscopes so valuable in navigation and stabilization systems. As I continued to shoot, my mind raced through the principles of physics at play. The bullet's spin, imparted by the rifling, created a gyroscopic effect that maintained its stability in flight. The faster the spin, the more stable the bullet's trajectory. It was a perfect example of angular momentum conservation in action.

Suddenly, as I watched another bullet speed towards the target, something clicked in my mind. The bullet's flight, its spin, its stability - it all reminded me of something else. Something cosmic. Stars. Planets. Galaxies.

The realization hit me like a thunderbolt. The same principles that governed the flight of this tiny bullet also applied to the grand celestial bodies that Professor Fitzgerald and his brother had spent their lives studying. The stability of a planet's orbit, the spin of a galaxy - these were all manifestations of the same physical laws I was observing on a microscopic scale here at the shooting range.

And then it struck me - $F_c$, the crucial variable in the Drake Equation that had eluded me for so long. $F_c$, the fraction of planets with life that goes on to develop a civilization capable of releasing detectable signs of their existence into space.

What if I had been thinking about it all wrong? What if, instead of looking at it as a simple fraction, we considered it as a function of stability? Just as a bullet's stability in flight depends on its spin and the forces acting upon it, perhaps the development of a civilization capable of interstellar communication too depends on the stability of its planet's orbit, its star system, even its galaxy.

My hands began to shake with excitement. I quickly put down the rifle and fumbled for my notebook in my bag pack. Scribbling furiously, I began to formulate a new approach to calculating $Fc$. It would involve considering factors we had previously overlooked - the galactic habitable zone, the stability of planetary orbits, the lifespan of parent stars.

As I wrote, I could almost hear Professor J. Fitzgerald's voice in my head, encouraging me, guiding me. This was it - the breakthrough we had been waiting for. By applying the principles of gyroscopic stability to celestial bodies, I could refine our estimate of $Fc$ and bring unprecedented precision to the Drake Equation.

I looked up from my notebook, my vision blurry from the intensity of my focus. As I fired another round, watching the bullet spiral towards the target, another realization struck me. The precision of the bullet's flight, its stability maintained by the rifling-induced spin, sparked a connection in my mind. It was as if the universe had aligned to show me something crucial about $FC$ - the fraction of planets with life that develops detectable technology. My hands trembled as I lowered the rifle. I fumbled for my notebook again, nearly dropping it in my excitement. The numbers began to flow, my pen barely able to keep up with my thoughts. If the stability of a bullet's flight could be quantified based on its spin and environmental factors, couldn't we apply a similar principle to planetary systems?

The stability of a planet's orbit, the consistency of its star's output, the protection offered by its magnetic field - all these factors would influence the likelihood of life developing advanced technology.

I scribbled furiously, developing a new formula that incorporated these elements.

As I worked, a number began to emerge - a specific value for *FC* that felt right, that resonated with everything I knew about astrophysics and the conditions necessary for life.

0.15. The number stared back at me from the page. Fifteen percent. It wasn't a guess or an approximation, but a value derived from concrete, observable phenomena. It represented the fraction of life-bearing planets that would go on to develop detectable technology, based on the stability of their environments. My heart raced as I stared at the number. This was it - the breakthrough I had been seeking. A specific, calculated value for *Fc* that could revolutionize our understanding of the Drake Equation and our place in the universe. I clutched the notebook to my chest, feeling the weight of this discovery. It wasn't just a number - it was a key to unlocking the mysteries of life in the cosmos, a tribute to the work of Jahangir Fitzgerald and Jawaharlal Fitzgerald, and a fulfilment of my own scientific journey. The words of Krishna once again echoed in my ears, *"Go forth and discover not just the secrets of the universe, but the depths of your own soul.....be ready when it comes to you."* The words seemed prophetic to me.

But that wasn't the end of my euphoria. The significance of *Fc's* value still reverberating through me, a strange stillness settled over the rifle range. The rhythmic pop of gunfire faded into the background, and for a moment, all I could hear was my own heartbeat.

0.15. The number for *FC* burned in my mind, a beacon of discovery. But as I stood there, something nagged at the edges of my consciousness. A whisper, barely audible: had I uncovered it all or was there more. Something I was missing. I glanced down at my notebook, my eyes tracing over the calculations that had led me to *FC*. And then, like a bolt of lightning, it struck me. My hands began to shake, and I nearly dropped the notebook. "Oh my God," I whispered, my voice trembling. *"Fi."*

The realization hit me with such force that I had to sit down, right there on the dusty ground of the rifle range. *Fi* - the fraction of planets with life where intelligence evolves. It had been there all along, hidden within the very same principles that had led me to *Fc*. With trembling hands, I reopened my notebook, flipping to a fresh page. My mind was racing, connections forming faster than I could process them. The same factors that influenced the development of technology - environmental stability, resource availability, planetary conditions - all played a role in the evolution of intelligence itself. I began to write feverishly, my pen barely keeping up with the flood of ideas. The formula for *fi* emerged as if it had a life of its own, building upon the foundations I'd laid with *FC* but taking on a unique shape. As I worked, I could feel the magnitude of what was happening.

This wasn't just a follow-up to my FC discovery. This was something equally monumental, equally world changing. Two of the most elusive variables in the Drake

Equation revealing themselves in rapid succession. When I finally reached the end of my calculations, I stared at the result in disbelief. There, at the bottom of the page, was a new number: 0.23.

I gasped audibly, drawing curious looks from nearby shooters. But I barely noticed them. *Fi* equalled 0.23. Twenty-three percent!

Planets with life would see the evolution of intelligence. The implications were staggering. In the span of a single afternoon, I had not only quantified *Fc* but also unlocked the value of *Fi*. Two crucial pieces of the cosmic puzzle, both springing from an unexpected moment of insight at a rifle range. Without help from Jawahar.

I looked up from my notebook, my vision blurry with unshed tears of excitement and disbelief. The world around me seemed to pulse with newfound significance.

Every blade of grass, every grain of sand, every distant star now held the potential for intelligent life in a way I had never fully grasped before. I was dumbfounded by the dual discovery. How I had come this far into the Equation!

Five.

That marked five of my horcruxes. And belief started entering me. I was going to do it. I was going to do something special, even though I hadn't yet. "I'm going to do it." I said to myself. And if one can see it in his mind, and contained the courage to speak it, it will happen. The Drake Equation will happen.

But I had to thank one man for it. One late afternoon sun hung low in the sky, casting long shadows across the shooting range. The air was thick with the acrid smell of gunpowder and the metallic tang of spent casings. I spotted him- the man I'd been searching for over the past month. Joe, the redneck I met during the marksman challenge at Berkeley, stood there, a solitary figure amidst the cacophony of gunfire. His weathered hands moved with practiced precision over an AK-47, adjusting sights and checking the magazine with a reverence that spoke of years of experience. As I approached, positioning myself in the adjacent lane, I could feel my heart racing, the weight of my recent discoveries - $Fc$ and $fi$ - pressing against my mind like a physical presence. Joe's eyes flickered towards me, sharp and observant despite the years etched into his face.

"Your breathing's too quick," he whispered, his voice barely audible over the staccato cracks of gunfire echoing around us. The words hung in the air, a gentle admonishment from a master to a novice. I inhaled deeply, trying to steady myself. The familiar scent of gun oil and leather filled my nostrils, grounding me in the present moment.

"Yes, I'm glad to see you at the range again," I replied, my fingers tracing the cool metal of the rifle before me. The texture was familiar, almost comforting, like greeting an old friend.

Joe nodded, a hint of a smile playing at the corners of his mouth. His accent was a curious mix - part southern drawl, part something I couldn't quite place. It was as if his voice itself was a puzzle, reflecting the enigma of the man.

"Joe," I repeated, my voice filled with a respect I hadn't anticipated. "I have to thank you. You've helped me in a way I cannot explain."

My words hung between us, and for a moment, I was tempted to share everything - the breakthroughs, the revelations that had reshaped my understanding of the universe. But the memory of Jehangir's fate flashed through my mind, a stark reminder of the dangers of sharing too much, too soon.

"You're welcome," Joe replied, his eyes crinkling with curiosity. They were a pale blue, like faded denim, and seemed to hold secrets of their own. "I bet it's something to do with rifles."

"Yes," I said, my response purposefully vague. The lie of omission sat uncomfortably on my chest, but I pushed on, changing the subject. "How do I become the best shooter in Berkeley?"

Joe chuckled, a low rumble that seemed to vibrate through the air, mixing with the distant thunder of gunfire. "I wouldn't know, son. I'm not a shooter myself. I'm an engineer - I design weapons, to the extent of my desire."

Fascination bloomed within me, pushing aside my earlier discomfort. I hefted the AK-47, feeling its weight distributed along my arms.

"That's amazing," I said, admiring at the balance of the weapon. "You have quite a hand. This feels so light."

Pride glimmered in Joe's eyes, like sunlight catching on still water. "Yeah, so what I basically did was hop on SolidWorks - a popular computer-aided design software - and imported sketches straight from the internet. But I decreased the weight-to-strength ratio." As he spoke, his hands moved in the air, sketching invisible diagrams. I could almost see the complex calculations and designs floating before us, a testament to the intricate dance between mathematics and engineering.

"Joe, you are quite the engineer," I gaped, my voice tinged with genuine admiration. "What makes you so interested in the applied sciences?"

He shrugged, a wry smile playing on his lips. The gesture was casual, but I sensed a depth of passion behind it. "I used to play video games up till three in the morning. First-person shooters, notably Counter-Strike, Fortnite, and even Call of Duty every now and then."

I winced internally, memories of pixelated violence flashing through my mind.

"Violent games, aren't they? I mean, I just can't bear so much blood and death... and blood and more blood. But to each their own." I paused, considering the irony of discussing virtual violence while surrounded by very real weapons.

"I also cannot design a weapon the way you can. I'm more inclined to the theoretical sciences."

"Oh?" Clint's eyebrows raised; curiosity evident in the slight tilt of his head. "What exactly interests you?"

"Astrophysics," I replied, unable to keep the excitement from my voice. As I spoke the word, my mind soared beyond the confines of the shooting range, out into the vast expanse of the cosmos.

Joe shook his head, his expression a mix of amusement and disbelief. The late afternoon sun caught the silver in his hair, creating a halo effect that seemed oddly fitting. "I can't study the sky if my life depended on it. I'm of the belief we should first understand our Earth. We've only explored a quarter of it. Can you believe that? And before the three/fourths left, people are insane enough to dig the moon first."

His words painted a vivid picture - the unexplored depths of our own planet juxtaposed against the barren lunar landscape. It was a perspective I hadn't considered, and for a moment, I felt the vastness of space shrink in comparison to the mysteries that lay beneath our feet. Joe paused, noticing my wide-eyed expression.

"But anyway, I didn't mean to alarm you."

"You didn't," I assured him, my mind still grappling with this new perspective.

Then, curiosity getting the better of me, I asked, "I've noticed you've spent so long in this shooting range. Have you never been interested in picking up one of your inventions and having a go yourself?" As soon as the words left my mouth, I saw a change come over Joe. His earlier confidence seemed to evaporate, replaced by a vulnerability that was almost palpable. His eyes darted nervously to the rifle in his hands, as if seeing it for the first time.

"I'm scared," he admitted, his voice barely above a whisper. The admission hung in the air between us, as loud as any gunshot.

"Scared?" I scoffed; my tone harsher than I intended. The cognitive dissonance – a weapons designer afraid to fire his own creations - struck me as absurd. "That's bollocks. Do you think the bullet is going to backfire and hit you in the nose when you squeeze? You should know your inventions better than that."

As soon as the words left my mouth, I regretted them. Joe's face had fallen, his earlier enthusiasm replaced by a look of hurt and embarrassment. The vibrant, passionate engineer I had been conversing with seemed to shrink before my eyes, and I realized my reaction had been born out of my own passion for the sport. Rifle shooting had been my metaphoric bread and butter - no, my bread, butter, and marmalade – at one point. The feel of the stock against my shoulder, the moment of perfect stillness before pulling the trigger, the satisfaction of a well-placed shot – these were as natural to me as breathing. I couldn't fathom finding it so daunting.

"I hit the bullseye once every three times at least," I said, trying to soften my earlier outburst. My words felt inadequate in the face of Joe's obvious discomfort. "Why can't you? We're both human, after all."

As silence fell between us, punctuated only by the distant pop of gunfire, I realized this exchange was unlike any I'd experienced before. At first, I had found Joe's mastery of computer design Goliath-like, insurmountable. His ability to manipulate digital space to create tangible, deadly objects was a skill so far removed from my own expertise that it seemed almost magical. Then he had found my mastery of rifle shooting a task he was too restless - or perhaps too fearful - to attempt. The very act that brought me clarity and focus was, for him, a source of anxiety and trepidation. We stood there, two sides of a coin, each pondering at the other's expertise while grappling with our own limitations. The late afternoon sun dipped lower, casting a golden glow across the range. Long shadows stretched from the firing stations, merging with the darker silhouettes of distant targets.

At that moment, surrounded by the acrid smell of gunpowder and the metallic gleam of firearms, I felt a strange kinship with this man - this engineer who could design weapons but feared to fire them.

Our worlds, so different yet intersecting in this unlikely place, seemed to vibrate with possibility. The crack of a distant shot broke the silence, making Joe flinch slightly. I watched as he composed himself, his engineer's mind visibly working to rationalize his fear. In his struggle, I saw a reflection of my own battles with the complexities of astrophysics, the moments of doubt and confusion that preceded each breakthrough.

I realized that our conversation had shifted something fundamental in my understanding. The universe, in all its vastness, was mirrored here in this small interaction - two humans, each brilliant in their own way, each limited by their own fears and biases, standing at the intersection of creation and destruction, theory and application.

The weight of $F_c$ and $F_i$ pressed against my mind once more, but now they seemed to take on new meaning. I felt I had stumbled upon another equation - one that spoke to the complex interplay of human knowledge, creativity, and fear. As I opened my mouth to speak again, to perhaps bridge the gap I had unknowingly created, I realized that this encounter with Joe was more than just a chance meeting. I continued our conversation: "What is it exactly about shooting that bothers you?" I asked, breaking the comfortable silence that had settled between us.

Joe's weathered face creased with thought. "I can't focus," he replied, his voice barely audible over the distant crack of gunfire. "All my life, I've been an overthinker. I look at simple things and twist them in a totally different direction."

He launched into an explanation, using the mundane act of watching paint dry as an example. Where others saw tedium, Joe saw an opportunity to ponder the deeper meanings of art, the true intentions behind a painting. His mind, it seemed, never rested. "Can you imagine being free of anything and everything?" he asked, his eyes distant. "Nothing can fear one who has no ability to experience emotions. And shooting... shooting takes habit and thought out of its equation."

I nodded, understandingly. "Yes, like me. Rifle shooting is not to be an Olympian, but to be a saint," I replied, thinking of the mental discipline required. "The same could be said about archery - two sports with similar foundations and ideology, but with different instruments." I asked Joe if he'd ever tried the sport. His response was unexpected and revealing.

"July 9th, if I recall correctly," he began, his voice tinged with a mix of embarrassment and frustration. "Four years ago, I took the rifle in my hand and aimed at the target. My eye was positioned perfectly, but the gun... it was moving in a frenzy, like a circular motion. My mind went ballistic." He went on to describe how he'd thrown the gun in anger, breaking it. The incident had cost him $9000 in fines, a sum he couldn't afford as a student already burdened with loans. But from this disaster came opportunity - he'd offered to build a replacement rifle, discovering his passion for Weaponry Engineering in the process.

"I spent the rest of my time building that AK you used today," Joe said, a hint of pride creeping into his voice. "I found my passion. Consequently, I received an admission into the Corps of Cadets military school at Berkeley, and now I pitch new designs directly to the U.S. military."

As Joe finished his story, I marvelled at how a moment of failure had led to such success. Yet, I couldn't help but wonder about the anger that had driven him to break the rifle in the first place.

"The virtue of patience scares you, more or less?" I asked, trying to understand.

Joe nodded, explaining how the difficulty of maintaining focus for even five minutes had been infuriating for his restless nature. "I've never been exposed to something so infuriatingly difficult, especially for a restless redneck like me," he admitted.

"You know, Joe," I began, my voice taking on a thoughtful tone, "rifle shooting is as much about the mind as it is about the eyes. It's about mastering both in perfect harmony." Clint leaned in, his curiosity palpable. I continued, "When I look at the target, I don't see concentric circles or numbers. I see only one perfect ring that spells '10 10'. It's like the rest of the world fades away, and there's only that ring, floating in space." I gestured towards the distant targets, now barely visible in the fading light. "To see the target like this, as others find impossible, is to enter a state of perfect focus. It's about training your eyes to see beyond what's physically there."

Joe's eyes widened, a mix of awe and disbelief playing across his features.

"Incredible," he breathed, shaking his head slightly. "How do you master your mind like that?"

I smiled, remembering my own journey to reach this level of mental control. "It's a process, Joe. It starts with breathing. Remember how you noticed my breathing was too quick earlier?" He nodded, hanging on every word. "Well, that's the first step. We have to learn to breathe normally, even when our heart is racing, and our palms are sweaty. It's about finding calm in the storm." I demonstrated, taking a deep, measured breath. "Then, it's about simplicity. We must keep things simple. While I stand in this range among some of the brightest, most skilled gunmen in the world, I realize my competition is not them, but me." Joe nodded slowly, understanding dawning in his eyes.

"I need to better myself to be the best," I continued, "I also couldn't care less about being the best. It's about the journey, the constant improvement." I paused, letting my words sink in. "In that moment of perfect focus, when the world narrows down to just you and the target, you realize that all your doubts, fears, and distractions are just... noise. They fall away, leaving only the purity of the shot."

Joe was silent for a long moment, processing what I'd said. When he spoke, his voice was filled with a newfound respect. "That's... that's beautiful. It's like you're describing a form of meditation, not just a sport."

I nodded, pleased that he'd grasped the essence of what I was trying to convey.

"Exactly, Joe. It's a meditation with a rifle. A dance between stillness and action, focus and release." As we stood there, the last light fading from the sky, I could see the wheels turning in Joe's mind. He was seeing shooting - and perhaps his own engineering work - in a new light. And in that moment, I realized that our exchange had opened new perspectives for both of us.

As we bid goodbye to each other, Joe said while parting, "All the best Sid. Do let me know if I can do anything for you."

Little did he know that he had been instrumental in helping me more than he thought. His one invitation of asking whether I could shoot had set me on the path of my hobby and my passion.

Later in the day I face-timed my family. It was time to reveal my discoveries to them. They were the people I could truly trust, irrespective of Jehangir's experience in life.

"I must tell you'll," I began, my voice low, "I've contained this part of me for some time, but I'll let it out now. I need to tell you'll about the Drake's equation and how far I have progressed."

My father's face showed surprise and interest. "What equation beta?"

I told them about the Drake Equation, about my lost professor and friend, and about the rekindled fire to solve this cosmic puzzle. I spoke of Sagan's "Cosmos" and the journey it had set Jahangir and Jawahar Fitzgerald on. As I talked, I could see the wonder growing in everyone's eyes.

"This is just beautiful," my sister said, awe evident in her voice. "Your mind must be so far advanced for you to even think about solving the equation. I wish there was a way we could help you. I truly do.

My Myomi stated proudly, "You... you've shown us there's so much more to see." She paused, struggling to find the right words. "This equation of yours, this... cosmic puzzle. It's beautiful. And I wish I could help you solve it."

I nodded, touched by her sincerity. "You'll already have mom. More than you'll know. Your support and love are the best inspiration for me"

A small smile played at the corners of Jay's, lips. "Maybe. But I think you're onto something big here. Something that could change everything."

Akash who had been silent so far finally spoke up, pride evident in his voice, "Sid let me give you one piece of advice, from one man to another - look where others may not."

The words hung in the air between us, simple yet profound. Eyes bored into mine, willing me to understand the depth of what he was trying to convey. "The answers you're seeking," he continued, "they might not be where you expect. Don't just look at the stars, or the numbers, or the theories. Look in the spaces between. In the quiet moments. In the things others overlook."

I nodded, beginning to grasp the full meaning of his words.

"The universe is vast," Dad chimed in, his voice barely above a whisper, "But so is the human mind. So is the realm of possibility. Don't limit yourself to the obvious paths Sid. Forge your own."

"And when you do solve that equation, when you unravel the mysteries of the cosmos, remember this moment. Remember that sometimes, the greatest insights come from the most unlikely places."

Much later, one sentence kept echoing in my mind… *"Look where others may not."* The words stayed with me, a mantra that would guide my research in the days, weeks, and months to come.

# Chapter 10

# EYE OF THE BIRD

In the days that followed, I found myself reflecting on my time at Berkeley. It wasn't just about guns and bullets and rednecks. There was a richness to life here that I hadn't fully appreciated before. I thought about the Holi festival celebrated by the Indian Student Association, how the vibrant colours - orange, blue, and green reminded me of home. The sense of community it fostered, bringing a piece of India to the United States, was palpable.

Yet, even amidst this celebration, I felt the absence of my family - my father's sophisticated nature, my sister in medical school, my brothers' reassuring presence, my mother's preservation of our traditions. I wondered where I could find these touchstones of my culture in the United States. "Mitti ki khushboo," *fragrance of home,* I murmured to myself, remembering the scent of home. In my uncompromising pursuit of precision, in this chase for glory, I realized I had lost track of my traditions, my culture and above all my people. As Rubik had told me in Budapest, this demand for perfection had made me forget how to be imperfect, how to be human. I resolved to find a balance between my scientific pursuits and my cultural roots, to remember that even in the quest for cosmic understanding, there was value in embracing the messy, imperfect nature of human existence.

The faces of those who had touched my life flashed before me - Avantika, Jawahar, Krishna, Ronald, Jehangir, and Joe. Each had appeared in my life for a reason, I was sure of it. These weren't mere coincidences, but pivotal moments in my journey. They were like my *Horcruxes.*

As I stood, the weight of the Drake Equation pressing on my mind, I realized that my path forward would require more than just scientific acumen. It would demand a synthesis of all I had learned - the precision of rifle shooting, the spirituality of life, the wonder of astrophysics, and the grounding force of my cultural heritage.

The golden tip of the temple pierced the California sky, a beacon of familiarity in this foreign land. As I approached, the scent of incense and flowers wafted through the air, stirring memories of home. Marigolds and jasmine adorned the entrance, their vibrant colours a stark contrast to the muted tones of Berkeley's academic buildings. I slipped off my shoes, feeling the cool stone beneath my feet. The rough texture grounded me, a tactile reminder of the countless devotees who had walked this path before. Inside, the air was thick with the smoke of burning *ghee* lamps, their flickering flames casting dancing shadows on the walls. The statue of Lord Vishnu loomed before me, its multiple arms seeming to embrace the entire cosmos. Each hand held a symbol - the conch, the discus, the lotus, the mace — each a universe of meaning unto itself. I stood there, overwhelmed by a sense of smallness in the face of eternity. The weight of my scientific pursuits felt insignificant in this ancient space. Suddenly, a rhythmic chanting broke the silence.

The sound reverberated through the temple, seeming to make the very air vibrate with its intensity. I turned to see a monk, his ash-smeared body a stark contrast to the colourful temple decorations. His eyes were closed in devotion, uttering words I couldn't quite catch. The cadence was hypnotic, drawing me in despite my initial shyness. Curiosity got the better of me.

"Excuse me," I whispered to a nearby priest, his saffron robes swaying as he turned to face me. "What is he saying?"

The priest's eyes crinkled as he smiled, his weathered face a map of devotion and wisdom. "He's not saying anything, my son. He cut out his tongue decades ago." I recoiled, shocked. The words hit me like a physical blow, my mind struggling to comprehend such an act.

"But... why?" I stammered, my voice a mix of horror and fascination.

"For moksha," the priest replied simply, as if discussing the weather.

"He saw Vishnu himself."

This was complete bonkers. I couldn't believe anyone bought into this. I had spent years learning about atoms, stars, and the laws of the universe. Everything had a logical explanation. Cutting out your tongue because you saw a god? That was just crazy talk. But that chanting... it was doing something weird to me. I could feel it in my chest, like a deep bass at a concert. It was just sound waves? So why did it feel so... powerful? None of this made any sense.

There was no scientific proof for any of it. These people were living in a superstitious world. They were throwing away reason for blind belief and moksha. God I could believe in – but this blind, irrational belief?

Suddenly the whole place seemed like a theme park for grown-ups who couldn't handle reality. It was embarrassing.

He saw Vishnu? Why did part of me want to believe it, even though I knew it was impossible? The rational part of my brain was screaming at me to leave, to run back to the safety of my equations and telescopes. This place, these beliefs - they were a threat to everything I had worked for, everything I thought I knew about the universe. As I stumbled out into the California sunshine, my head spun with conflicting thoughts. The Western rationality I'd embraced at Berkeley clashed violently with the mysticism I'd just witnessed. The golden arches of a McDonald's in the distance seemed garish and out of place after the timeless beauty of the temple. I felt torn between two worlds, unsure of where I truly belonged. Was I the devoted Hindu son my parents had raised, or the sceptical scientist Berkeley had shaped me into? The question echoed in my mind, drowning out the noise of passing cars and chattering students.

That night, I tossed and turned in my bed, images of the tongueless monk mixing with equations and star charts in my dreams. The Drake Equation seemed both vitally important and utterly meaningless in the face of such unwavering faith. I drifted in and out of consciousness, my mind a battlefield of conflicting ideologies.

Suddenly, a hand shook me awake. The touch was firm yet gentle, impossibly real for what, to this day, I do not know was a dream or not. I opened my eyes to pitch darkness. A figure stood by my bed, emanating a soft, impossible light. The glow seemed to come from within, illuminating a face I had seen countless times in paintings and statues.

"Arjuna?" I whispered, hardly daring to believe it. My voice sounded small in the darkness, a child's voice full of wonder and fear. The air in the room felt charged, as if the laws of physics themselves were holding their breath in anticipation. Here, in my small Berkeley apartment, worlds were colliding - science and faith, past and present, the cosmic and the deeply personal.

As the demigod opened his mouth to speak, my entire body froze.

Arjuna was there, glowing softly in the darkness of my room. My heart pounded so hard I could hear it in my ears. Sweat broke out across my forehead. I wanted to run, to scream, to call someone - anyone. But I couldn't move. Couldn't speak. I was trapped between terror and awe, my scientific mind waging war against what my eyes were telling me. Everything I had learned, everything I thought I knew, was about to be challenged. The quest for knowledge that had driven me across oceans and through years of study suddenly seemed small, almost childish, in the face of this cosmic impossibility. I struggled to breathe, to think clearly.

"I am Arjuna, son of Indra, devotee of Krishna, warrior of Lord Shiva." His words hung in the air, echoing like a distant drumbeat in my mind. As they left his mouth, I felt a shudder pass through my body. This wasn't possible. I could hardly believe what was happening right in front of me. I, Siddhant, an astrophysicist who believed in reason and science. Yet here I was, facing a figure out of legend.

I struggled to find my voice, my thoughts a jumbled mess of doubt and wonder.

"But... but how? Why are you here, speaking to me? This can't be real."

Arjuna smiled, a serene expression that seemed to hold the weight of countless lifetimes. "Why does it surprise you, Siddhant? You have come so far, carried such big dreams. To serve your people, to find the truth in the stars. You have sought answers that many seek but few understand."

His voice was calm, each word measured, as if he had all the time in the world. There was a certainty in his tone that unsettled me, a deep truth that I couldn't deny, no matter how much I wanted to.

"Isn't that what you wanted? To serve? To understand the universe and our place within it?"

I swallowed; my throat dry. "I... I suppose so. But Arjuna, you're a myth, a legend. How can you be here now? Why now?"

Arjuna's eyes softened, and he stepped closer. I could feel his presence like a warm breeze, tangible and real. "Just as a devotee is incomplete without his God, so also God is incomplete without his true *bhakt*. I am here, Siddhant, because you have called me. Maybe not with your words, but with your actions, your thoughts, your quest for truth. You see me on TV, in films, in books, and calendars, but I am more than those images. I am a living, breathing being, just like you. And I have a message for you."

I shook my head, still grappling with the reality of the moment.

"But why me? I'm just a scientist. I believe in science."

Arjuna's expression didn't change; if anything, it grew more understanding.

"*Aastha*, or faith, isn't about belief in Gods, Siddhant. It is about belief in something greater than oneself, a purpose, a path. You believe in science, and that is your faith. Those who listen to others and decide for themselves that there is no God are still guided by faith—the faith that their understanding, their logic, is correct."

His words struck a chord deep within me. I had always seen faith as something religious, something outside the realm of reason. Yet here was Arjuna, a symbol of faith, telling me that my belief in science was a form of faith too.

"I... I've never thought of it that way," I admitted, my voice barely more than a whisper.

"That's why I'm here," Arjuna said, his voice gentle but firm. "To show you that science and faith are not opposites, but parts of the same whole. The universe is vast, Siddhant. It is filled with wonders and mysteries beyond human understanding. You have spent your life searching for answers, but sometimes, answers come in ways you do not expect."

I took a deep breath, trying to steady myself. "What do you want me to do? What is this message you are conveying?"

Arjuna's gaze was intense, his eyes locking onto mine. "The world is one family, Siddhant. I have travelled to infinite worlds, and I have not seen one quite like this. Your people, your friends, your family—they are all connected. And so are you. You are not alone in this vast universe. There are others like you, others who seek knowledge, who strive to understand. You have been chosen to carry this message, to be a bridge between science and faith, between the known and the unknown."

His words filled me with a sense of awe and responsibility. I had always felt that my work, my pursuit of knowledge, was important. But now, it seemed like it was part of something much bigger than myself.

"I... I'll try," I said, my voice trembling with the weight of the moment. "But I'm just one person. How can I make a difference?"

Arjuna smiled, his expression warm and reassuring. "You are not just one person, Siddhant. You are a spark, a catalyst for change. And you are not alone. There are others like you, others who will hear your message and be inspired by your journey. Remember, even the smallest of actions can create ripples that change the course of history."

Arjuna placed a hand on my shoulder, his touch light but reassuring.

"That is all anyone can ask for, Siddhant. To do their best, to follow their path with honesty and courage. Remember, you are never alone. I will be with you, guiding you, just as Krishna guided me."

With those words, Arjuna stepped back, his form beginning to shimmer and fade. I reached out, wanting to hold onto the moment, to keep him with me a little longer.

"Wait!" I called; my voice filled with urgency. "Before you go, tell me one thing.

Are there really more out there? More worlds, more life?" Arjuna's form wavered, but his voice remained steady. "The universe is infinite, Siddhant. And so are its possibilities. Never stop searching, never stop questioning. The truth is out there, waiting to be discovered."

And with that, he was gone.

I woke up with a start, realising it was all a dream. No, I may have been asleep, but it wasn't a dream. It was a vision. A greater power shining a beacon for me.

I recollected the words spoken. It filled me with a sense of wonder and purpose. The universe was vast, infinite, and filled with possibilities. And I, Siddhant, was a part of it all, a seeker of truth in a world of endless mysteries. I stood there for a long time, my mind racing with thoughts and ideas. The night sky stretched out above me, a canvas of stars that seemed to go on forever. I had been given a gift, a chance to see the world in a new light, to understand the connection between science and faith. And I would not squander it. I would follow my path, wherever it might lead, knowing that I was not alone. Arjuna's words echoed in my mind, a constant reminder of the journey that lay ahead. As I reflected on the words, it became clear to me that the value of $Ne$ was not a fixed number but an ever-expanding concept. The universe, with its limitless possibilities, held countless forms of life in ways beyond our current understanding. $Ne$, the number of habitable exoplanets, was infinite, just like the universe itself. This realization changed everything, as I understood that the search for extra-terrestrial life was truly a journey into the boundless nature of existence.

Arjuna had given me my 7th and ultimate Horcrux and left.

I could feel the thrill of a Nobel Peace Prize in my bones, a sense of achievement that filled every part of my being.

At the tender age of 17, I was told that I couldn't finish the equation. Yet here I was at 24, having determined six of the seven critical values. The weight of that accomplishment was both thrilling and terrifying. The final value, the one last piece of the puzzle, was all that stood between me and the answer I had sought for years. All I wanted was someone to verify whether I was right or wrong because, in science, there are a million possibilities, but only one of them is infinitely correct. I had no way to cross-check my work against anyone else's, and that uncertainty gnawed at me. But then, I remembered Professor Fitzgerald. He had six values before he died, the same six I had now uncovered. For the first time, I felt we were standing on equal ground. Professor Fitzgerald had been more than just a mentor; he was a father figure, a guiding star. His belief in me had sparked my interest in astrophysics, and now, I was on the brink of completing what he had started. I just needed that one final step for him, for his brother, and for myself.

"Eye of the bird," I murmured to myself, remembering prof. Fitzgerald's cryptic message. The phrase replayed in my mind, disentangling itself with each repetition. I could hear voices in my head, urging me to find the last piece of the puzzle. Arjuna had said to add perspective into things, to go back to my roots. And I finally understood. My roots were where it all began—with Professor Fitzgerald, on the rooftop of his building, where we would observe the night sky through our telescope, the one I had built with my own hands. He had seen the bigger picture, a perspective from above, where everything came into focus. A bird, I realized, sees everything from above. Its perspective is all-encompassing, an isometric view that captures every detail from the top down. That was the clue I needed. Arjuna had told me to go back to my roots, and my roots were on that rooftop, where a bird could see as it flies high in the sky.

The message was clear: to understand the final value, I needed to see things from a higher perspective, literally and figuratively. I had to see beyond the numbers and the data, to look at the universe from the vantage point of the telescope, where the journey had begun. The answer lay in the perspective—seeing the world from above, as a bird would, taking in everything from a higher vantage point.

That's when it occurred to me.

"THE VALUES ARE INSIDE THE TELESCOPE," I screamed.

They weren't just abstract concepts or distant stars; they were right there, inside the telescope, where the bird's eye view truly mattered. I had built the telescope with my own hands, each piece carefully crafted, every lens precisely positioned. It reflected my journey, my dedication, my pursuit of the truth. And it was positioned on the terrace, where a bird's eye sees the world in its entirety. Fitzgerald's message, "Eye of the bird," suddenly made perfect sense. The telescope was more than just a tool; it was the key to seeing what others couldn't, to finding the perspective that had eluded me all this time. It was there, under the vast sky, that I would uncover the final piece of the puzzle. This realization struck me with the force of a revelation. The variables—the secrets of the universe, the truths I had been searching for—were embedded in the very instrument I had created. The telescope, with its bird's eye view, was not just a portal to the stars; it was a gateway to understanding. To see through its lens was to see from the perspective of a bird, to witness the universe as a connected, infinite whole. The final step wasn't out there in the cosmos; it was where it all began, professor's and my observatory: His building's rooftop.

My heart raced as I grabbed my bag and rushed out of my room, heading straight for the airport. This was it—the culmination of years of work, dreams, and unrelenting pursuit. The words "eye of the bird" had haunted me for as long as I could remember, a riddle whose answer now felt within reach. I recalled the shooting stars I had seen at Kamyakavana and the wish I had made that night: to back my intuition and find the truth. I had followed that intuition across continents and years, and now, it was leading me back to Mumbai, back to where it all began.

Seventeen hours of travel felt like a lifetime. My thoughts drifted to Professor Fitzgerald, to the countless nights we had spent on his rooftop, gazing at the stars. Those were the nights that had shaped my dreams, that had set me on this path. I wondered what he would think of me now, chasing a revelation across the globe.

Would he have been proud of the man I had become, of the scientist who dared to believe in the impossible?

Each hour that passed seemed to stretch into eternity. I couldn't help but think of all the years I had devoted to this quest, the sleepless nights spent pouring over equations, the countless times I had doubted myself. My mind replayed every lecture, every conversation with Fitzgerald, every time he had challenged me to think beyond the conventional. His voice echoed in my head, reminding me to look at the universe not just through the eyes of a scientist, but with the curiosity and wonder of a child.

As I stormed through the doors of Professor Fitzgerald's building, I felt a surge of memories. The elevator ride to the topmost floor was a journey through time, each floor a chapter of my life. My heart pounded as I recalled all the times I had entered this building, filled with doubts and questions. "Professor, what about light behaving not only as a particle but also as a wave? How can I model a graph of the blue star exploding?" I had bombarded him with questions, each one a steppingstone on my path to discovery. He would clear all my doubts away, his patience as vast as the cosmos itself. The elevator bell rang, "30", jolting me back to the present. I stepped onto the rooftop, my heart in my throat. The sight of our equipment, untouched and pristine, filled me with a sense of nostalgia. The big old Kalman tracker stood as it always had, a sentinel to our nights of stargazing. The solar flare receiver was a little dusty, but it could still be as good as new with a little work. And there it was—the telescope, the relic of the Hubble Space Telescope, the one I had painstakingly built to prove my worth to Professor Fitzgerald.

It had been my labour of love, a testament to my capabilities, and he had been proud of me, though he rarely showed it. His approval had always been silent, a nod here, a smile there, but his actions spoke louder than words. He had saved his work, our work, for me. The telescope stood as a symbol of my journey, of the bond between us that transcended life and death. I ran my fingers along its surface, feeling the cool metal beneath my skin. It was as if I could feel professor's presence beside me, guiding me one last time. I adjusted the telescope, aiming it at the stars, just as we had done countless times before. I walked toward the telescope, nervous and excited. My heart pounded in my chest, each step echoing with the significance of this moment. I had come halfway across the world for this, to find the answers that had eluded me for so long. As I reached the telescope, I hesitated for a second, then opened the tip, expecting to find something inside— anything that would point me in the right direction. But there was nothing. My heart sank. Did I come all this way for nothing? I scanned every part of the telescope, my hands running over its cold metal surface, feeling every groove, every screw. It was just as I had left it, the same telescope I had built with Professor Fitzgerald all those years ago. I walked all over the terrace, searching for any sign of the variables, anything that would give me a clue. But there was nothing. The terrace was empty, save for the telescope and the memories it held.

Had my intuition been wrong? Had I misinterpreted Arjuna's message? Frustrated, I turned back to the telescope. It seemed to mock me, standing there silently under the night sky. But then, a thought crossed my mind. Perhaps I had been looking in the wrong place all along. I approached the telescope one final time, this time not searching its surface, but looking through it. I placed my eye against the eyepiece, ready to view the night sky, expecting to see the familiar stars. But instead, I saw something far more profound.

Through the lens, the night sky blurred and shifted, revealing not stars, but numbers—variables. *Fp: 0.2, R*: 365 per days, Fi: 2.3, Fl: 5.7724, Fc; 0.12, Ne: infinity*. Each one glowing softly, as if written in light. I could hardly believe my eyes. The variables were there, floating in the darkness, just as prof. Fitzgerald had always envisioned. It was as if the telescope had transformed, becoming a bridge between the known and the unknown. I saw the values of each variable, each one perfectly aligned with the ones I had calculated. And then, there it was—L, the value I had been searching for, the final piece of the puzzle. When I turned the bolt after the sixth variable, Ne, I saw a blue star.

"Wait a minute. Isn't that the star that collapsed?" I spoke to myself. I remembered when I went running to professor asking him how a blue star just vanished. It was Regulus. "Oh, Regulus' been there for about 10000 years Sid." Professor had told me. And that was it. My life came full circle. Watching Regulus had ignited the astrophysical flame in me. And Regulus took me across the final stage. *L*, average life of stars, is 10000.

In that moment, everything made sense. The telescope was the key, the means to see beyond the limits of the naked eye, to perceive the universe as a whole.

Professor Fitzgerald had known I would come here eventually. He had known that I would find my way back to this place, to the rooftop where it all began. It was as if he had left a part of himself in the telescope, a legacy for me to uncover. The realization washed over me; a wave of understanding that left me breathless. L— the value representing the longevity of civilizations, the measure of how long they can communicate across the stars— was infinite. It was the culmination of everything we had worked for, everything Fitzgerald had believed in. It was the understanding that life, in all its forms, had the potential to endure, to persist beyond the boundaries of time and space. As I stood there, the telescope still pressed against my eye, I felt a deep connection to prof. Fitzgerald. I liked to think that it was Dronacharya, Arjuna's guru, who had come to Professor Fitzgerald in his dreams, guiding him to the discovery of Ne. It wasn't the end of my journey; it was the beginning of something far greater. Fitzgerald's dream had become my reality, and together, we had uncovered the infinite possibilities of the universe.

And If I were ever standing in a forest, clouds covering the sky, a wooden bird partly hidden by foliage before me, and someone asked me what I saw, I'd say, "Eye of the Bird."